'What is it you'd like to know about my love-life, Dr O'Neill?' Andrew drawled.

'Of course I'm not the slightest bit interested,' Caitlin said, flustered. 'It was just a friendly question from one colleague to another. I'm assuming that we *can* be friends?'

He leaned forward. 'I don't know, Caitlin. What do you think?' he said softly.

He left Caitlin sitting, her heart thudding in the most disconcerting manner. She felt she had been thrown a challenge, but whatever it was she couldn't be sure.

Somehow, the only thing she felt sure of was that no man had ever made her feel like this before. Perhaps the safest course was to keep as far away from Dr Andrew Bedi as possible. And the safe course was always what Caitlin preferred.

Anne Fraser was born in Scotland, but brought up in South Africa. After she left school she returned to the birthplace of her parents, the remote Western Islands of Scotland. She left there to train as a nurse, before going on to university to study English Literature. After the birth of her first child, she and her doctor husband travelled the world, working in rural Africa, Australia and Northern Canada. Anne still works in the health sector. To relax, she enjoys spending time with her family, reading, walking and travelling.

Recent titles by the same author:

FALLING FOR HER MEDITERRANEAN BOSS
POSH DOC CLAIMS HIS BRIDE
HER VERY SPECIAL BOSS
DR CAMPBELL'S SECRET SON

THE PLAYBOY DOCTOR'S SURPRISE PROPOSAL

BY
ANNE FRASER

MILLS & BOON

First published in Great Britain 2009
Large Print edition 2010
Harlequin Mills & Boon Limited,
Eton House, 18-24 Paradise Road,
Richmond, Surrey TW9 1SR

© Anne Fraser 2009

ISBN: 978 0 263 21075 0

Harlequin Mills & Boon policy is to use papers that are
natural, renewable and recyclable products and made
from wood grown in sustainable forests. The logging and
manufacturing process conform to the legal environmental
regulations of the country of origin.

Printed and bound in Great Britain
by CPI Antony Rowe, Chippenham, Wiltshire

THE PLAYBOY DOCTOR'S SURPRISE PROPOSAL

CHAPTER ONE

HE PLUCKED her out of the sea. One minute she was floundering in the water, the next she was being manhandled to shore by a stranger with bronzed muscles and nutmeg-coloured eyes. It was by far the most embarrassing thing that had happened to her for as long as she could remember.

Ten minutes earlier, Caitlin had plunged into the Pacific, gasping as the cold water chased the heat of the Australian sun from her skin. She had ploughed through the water for a few moments until life had returned to her frozen limbs, then turned on her back and floated.

Her sister, Brianna, and the rest of the group were on the beach. Niall was fussing around lighting the barbecue, while Brianna relaxed with a book. The children were making sandcastles on the startlingly white sand, and the sounds of their laughter drifted over to Caitlin on the perfectly still air. She could still scarcely believe that she was here in Brisbane. Months of planning followed by a forty-eight-hour journey from Dublin and finally here she was. She only wished her trip could have been made under happier circumstances. Flipping over onto her stomach, she swam for a few more minutes, then trod water. Brianna's husband, Niall, had promised her that she was safe from sharks this close to shore, but Caitlin wasn't going to take any chances. She'd keep the beach within easy distance.

Looking towards the shore, she could see Niall and Brianna waving to her. Without her glasses, they were slightly fuzzy shapes against the glaring white of the sand. Caitlin waved back. Just a few more minutes then she'd return to shore and help her sister with lunch.

Her stomach gave the familiar flutter of anxiety that she always experienced these days when she thought about her older sister. Although Brianna was recovering well from her treatment, the sight of her nearly bald head with the wispy tendrils of hair had brought tears to Caitlin's eyes when she had first seen her at the airport. It had taken all her resolve not to show how shocked she was when she had hugged her sister and felt the fragile bones. Still she was here now. When she wasn't working, she'd be around to help, at the very least offer moral support.

The next time she looked up the beach had receded. She became aware that Brianna and Niall were still waving and Caitlin waved back again. They probably wanted her back on shore.

Flipping over on her stomach once more, she struck off towards the beach. She was a good swimmer, managing twenty lengths most mornings at her local pool before she left for work. Caitlin believed that routine and discipline were essential parts of life.

Stopping for a moment, she lifted her head out of the water to check the distance to the beach. To her dismay, she didn't seem to have made any progress. In fact, if it was possible, she appeared to have moved away from the shore and further out to sea. For the first time, Caitlin felt a flutter of anxiety. Niall had warned her about the currents but she hadn't paid too much attention, putting his concerns down to him being an anxious brother-in-law. Now, she realised grimly that he hadn't exaggerated. Clearly she was caught in a current that was dragging her out to sea. She felt the first flicker of real alarm.

She had read somewhere that the best thing to do was to swim across the current rather than against it. That way you'd eventually reach a point where the current would disappear. From there it should be easy to swim back.

By this time Niall had waded in up to his thighs and was gesticulating wildly. He had been joined by another figure, and although it was too far for Caitlin to see more than blurry outlines, she could see enough to know that the figure was tall, topping Niall by a good couple of inches, although her brother-in-law was no slouch in the height stakes. Caitlin had just enough time to wonder if the new figure was Andrew, her new colleague, who she'd been told was to join them for lunch, before she started swimming again.

Don't panic, she told herself as she cut through the water. *You've been in difficult situations before, and panicking never did anyone any good. Just swim parallel to the beach and everything will be fine. Eventually.*

She had only been swimming for another couple of minutes, but already she could feel the energy sapping out of her limbs. Swimming in the safe confines of her local pool was not the same thing as swimming in the sea. If she were to make it back safely she would need to conserve her energy. She would tread water for a few moments, just long enough to get her breath back, then start swimming again. She shuddered as she saw a mass of translucent blobs float past her. That was all she needed—jellyfish. She'd been told that Australian jellyfish could be lethal, along with hundreds of other snakes, sharks, spiders and goodness knew what else that seemed to favour the continent. And Caitlin didn't do dangerous animals. But typical of the way her luck had being going lately, she felt a sudden pain in her calf, as if she'd been stung by a thousand wasps. She cried out in pain and shock, swallowing water, and as she grabbed her leg, she felt herself go under.

She popped up again, gasping and choking. Now she was really worried. What if she had only a few minutes to live? One way or another right now her chances of survival seemed grim. At that moment she felt something touch her shoulder. What now? She twisted her body round to face this new threat and found herself looking into a pair of unfamiliar brown eyes. She guessed immediately it was the man she had seen standing with Niall.

'I've always wanted to rescue a damsel in distress,' he drawled. His wide grin made Caitlin furious. What on earth did he find amusing about her situation? Couldn't he see she was in trouble?

'I need to get ashore,' she panted. 'I've been stung.' She spluttered as a wave rolled over her, forcing more salt water down her already choked-up throat.

Hands reached for her. All trace of amusement vanished. 'Just do as I tell you and don't fight me,' he said, his deep voice calm. 'Just roll over onto your back and relax. I'll take you in.'

Caitlin hesitated. Despite her terror there was no way she was going to be dragged ashore like so much flotsam.

'Or, so help me, I'll knock you out if I have to,' he threatened as if he read her mind.

The hardness in his tone made Caitlin realise he was deadly serious. He would knock her out—she didn't doubt him for a second! The last thing she had the strength for was a brawl. And she did need help. Her leg was agonising and she was finding it difficult to breathe. Giving up all pretence of being able to get herself out of her predicament, she rolled over on her back and let herself float. She felt firm hands grasp either side of her head, and then she was being tugged towards the shore.

It could have only taken a few minutes but, exhausted and mortified, it felt like hours to Caitlin before she was being helped up the beach and onto a blanket. She dropped to her knees while Brianna dropped a towel around her shoulders.

'My God, Cat. Are you all right?' Brianna pressed a tumbler of water to her lips and Caitlin drank the liquid gratefully, washing away the taste of sea water. Over her sister's shoulder, Caitlin was conscious of the curious gazes of her niece and nephew. She shivered, trying to catch her breath, acutely aware how close she had come to being swept out to sea. Her rescuer knelt beside her and to her consternation gently lifted her calf and examined the place where she had been stung. Caitlin had the briefest impression of broad shoulders the colour of toffee and thick black hair.

'How's her leg, Andrew?' Niall asked, sounding concerned.

'It'll be okay. As soon as I get some vinegar on it.'

Caitlin's embarrassment deepened. So she'd been right. The man who had been forced to come after her to bring her ashore as if she were some helpless female was her new colleague. Dr Andrew Bedi. What a way to make a good first impression, she berated herself. He must think her all kinds of an idiot.

'I've got some vinegar in the boot of my car. If you could fetch it, Niall?' Andrew continued. He turned to Caitlin and smiled sympathetically.

'They're always getting me. It will sting like crazy for a while, but I don't think there's any lasting damage. You're lucky that you got stung by these babies. Now, if it had been the ones up north, you'd really be in trouble.' He raised his eyes to Caitlin's and once again she was aware of the intensity of his gaze. She felt a tingle in her leg, but whether it was from the feel of his hands or the shock of her recent experience, she didn't want to know. He was tall, at least six feet four, with short black hair. He was only wearing Bermuda shorts and Caitlin was acutely aware of his bronzed, muscular chest. Deep brown eyes, framed by impossibly thick lashes, glinted as if he found the whole world amusing. His features were perfectly sculpted, high cheek-bones and a full, generous mouth. People might have called him beautiful, if it weren't for his nose, which looked as if it had been broken and badly set. He was simply by far the sexiest man Brianna had ever seen—and she was to be working with him!

'Did no one warn you not to go too far out?' he said, frowning at her. Although he looked as if he was of Indian descent, his accent was Australian.

Caitlin prickled at the disapproval in his voice. She wasn't used to people telling her off. 'Yes. But I didn't notice how far the current had taken me until it was too late.' Caitlin pulled her leg out of his grasp, annoyed. Okay, so he'd had to rescue her, that was embarrassing and she owed him, but there was no need for him to talk to her as if she were a naughty child. 'Thank you for helping me out. I am very grateful…' She was aware that she sounded less than appreciative, but she desperately wanted to regain some dignity as quickly as possible. She wasn't used to feeling at a disadvantage, as if she was in the wrong. 'And I can promise you, I will never ever put myself, or any one else, in that position again. Okay?' She tried a smile and tugged her leg from his grasp. It was still stinging like hell, but she would just have to grit her teeth until the pain subsided.

'Oh, Caitlin,' Brianna was saying as Niall returned carrying a large brown leather bag. 'You gave us all such a fright.'

Caitlin hugged her sister. 'I'm sorry, sis. Particularly seeing as it's me that's supposed to be watching out for you.'

'Anyway, all's well that ends well,' Andrew said, taking the bag from Niall. After hunting around for a few moments, he pulled out a bottle and a dressing. He reached for Caitlin's leg once more and propped it on his knees. Caitlin was deeply aware of the heat of his skin on hers. Once again there was that tingle. Dismayed, she tried to pull her leg away again. Equally determined, he pulled it back and held it there with a steel-like grip. Caitlin gave up, knowing that if she entered into a tug of war with this man she was likely to come out the loser, and would look even sillier than she felt right now.

He glanced up at her and Caitlin could see laughter in his deep brown eyes. 'Just do as you're told for a few minutes,' he drawled. 'Brianna did warn me that you were a stubborn woman. Goes with the red hair, I guess.' He looked from Brianna to Caitlin. They both had auburn hair—or at least until Brianna's had fallen out as a side effect of her treatment. But where Brianna's hair had been a mass of curls, Caitlin wore hers longer, tamed into a silky curtain of thick waves. But adding to her discomfort, Caitlin was conscious that as her hair dried in the heat of the sun it was beginning to frizz. At the moment she was as far away from the sleek professional she liked to present to the world as was possible.

'I did not!' Brianna protested. 'I said she was determined—not stubborn.'

'Well I guess we both know who the other is, then,' Caitlin said, feeling ridiculous as she held out her hand. She in her bikini, frizzing hair plastered to her scalp, her leg in the lap of her colleague and now here she was holding out her hand as if they had just met at some cocktail party. It was so ludicrous she had to smile.

'Dr Caitlin O'Neill,' she said with a grin.

He stopped what he was doing for a moment and engulfed her hand in his. 'Dr Andrew Bedi. At your service.' Then he too smiled. The effect was devastating. His teeth were a flash of white against the darkness of his skin, his dancing eyes crinkled at the corners. He really was the most incredible-looking man. Caitlin's pulse, which had been beginning to resume its normal rhythm, uncomfortably started pounding again.

Eventually, having dressed her leg, he placed it back on the blanket. 'It'll feel a little bruised,' he said, 'and might be sore for a day or two, but that's all. You've been lucky. If it had been one of the brutes up the coast a bit that had stung you, you'd have been a goner for sure.'

Caitlin shuddered, her gaze shifting to the clear blue Pacific. There was no way she was going back in there unless she was sure it was perfectly safe. Once stung twice shy.

'I think we should go back to the house,' Niall said. 'And have our barbie there. Andrew, if you could take the girls, I'll follow with the kids once I've packed up here.'

'Please don't,' Caitlin said. 'I don't want to spoil everyone's day. If Andrew thinks my leg is okay, we should just carry on as if nothing has happened. C'mon, Niall. Please. I don't want to spoil it for everyone.'

'Yes, Daddy. Let's stay,' Caitlin's nephew,

Ciaran, begged. 'We haven't been down to the beach since Mummy got sick. And Siobhan and I have only half finished our castle.'

Caitlin was stricken with remorse. She was supposed to be here to help make things easier for the family. Now it looked as if she had ruined their first proper day out.

'I insist we stay,' she said firmly. 'Brianna and I will lie on the blanket here and chat. We still need to catch up properly. And as Andrew said, my leg will be perfectly fine.'

'Yippee,' Siobhan yelled in delight. 'Uncle Andrew was going to show us his tricks on his board. Now he can.' Now the drama was over, the little girl flung herself at Andrew, who pretended to be knocked over. He fell back in the sand, taking Siobhan with him. Seconds later, Ciaran had jumped on top of him too. Andrew seemed used to this behaviour. After a few minutes of horseplay he picked up Siobhan and threw her over his shoulder.

'C'mon, then. You kids can help me get my board set up. Your dad has to help too.'

As the two men walked away, two excited

children off their shoulders, Brianna turned to Caitlin.

'Well, what do you think?' she said, her green-grey eyes twinkling.

'About what?' Caitlin replied, although she knew full well what her sister meant.

Brianna smacked Caitlin playfully on the shoulder.

'About Andrew, of course.'

'What about him? He seems very nice. Rescuing me and all that. Very civil of him,' Caitlin said dryly.

'C'mon, Cat,' Brianna said warningly. 'Don't you think he's gorgeous?'

'I suppose some people would think he's good looking,' Caitlin replied slowly, studiously ignoring her sister's look of incredulity. 'But he's a bit Crocodile Dundee for my liking.'

'I don't believe you don't find him sexy as hell,' Brianna retorted. 'Every single woman I have ever seen meet him gets that same ga-ga look as you have. It's written all over your face.'

'Okay.' Caitlin laughed. 'He's a hunk. But he's so not my type.'

Her sister sighed. 'Just as well, I suppose, because I hate to tell you, sis, you haven't a hope as far as Dr Andrew Bedi is concerned.'

Caitlin popped a sun hat on her head and scrabbled around for her glasses. The world swam back into focus. Andrew, Niall and the two children had returned to the beach carrying a board and a sail. It looked like a windsurfing board to Caitlin, although she wasn't an expert. Andrew had pulled on a wetsuit over his Bermuda shorts and the fabric clung to his body, emphasising his height and muscular build.

'Why do you say that?' Caitlin asked. 'Not that I'm remotely interested, of course.' The two sisters shared a smile. 'You know me, Bri, I'm much too happy with my life as it is to want to get involved. Men and kids aren't part of the plan. Not for a few years anyway. But I'm a bit offended that you think I haven't a chance. What makes you think he's so out of my league?'

Caitlin had never really thought about whether men found her attractive. She had been happy with David for the last few years and, until a few weeks ago, had thought that one day they would marry. Undemanding and not the least bit resentful of the time she spent at work, they had rubbed along well enough. And if it hadn't been the most exciting relationship, at least it had been comfortable. However, Caitlin had been surprised at how easily they had parted when she'd told him she was coming to Brisbane for six months. David had told her that she was mad to jeopardise her career just when it was really taking off. But to Caitlin there was no competition. Her sister needed her and that was that. They had split up with surprisingly little regret on either side.

'Oh, you'll find out about Andrew in good time. But let's just say he's a man who likes women and seems determined to have as much fun with as many as possible before settling down—if he ever does. And you, my darling sister, are far too serious for a fun-loving guy like him.'

Caitlin let out a low whistle, then wrinkled her nose disapprovingly. She looked over to the water's edge. Niall and Andrew had rigged the sail on the board and were pointing it towards the sea. Then with a push of his foot, Andrew was on the water and heading out away from the shore. Within seconds he was racing across the sea. With her glasses back in place, Caitlin could see him attach something that looked like a rope to the sail and then, as he leant back, the board seemed to leap forward, skimming over the waves. Within minutes he was a speck on the horizon.

'No, you're right. Men like Andrew have never appealed to me. If I marry, it will be to someone who likes the same things I do. Someone solid and steady.'

'Someone boring, you mean. Like David. That didn't work very well either.' Brianna laughed.

Brianna had met David on the one occasion she and her family had come back to Ireland for a visit to show off the children to their mother when Ciaran had been two. Caitlin realised that they had never discussed David. She'd assumed Brianna had liked him. Everyone did.

'Hey, you never said you didn't like David. I thought you two hit it off.'

'I didn't say I didn't like him, Cat. I just never thought he was right for you. If you ask me, he squeezed the fun right out of everything. You two were like a couple who had been married for years. You never really struck me as two people in love.'

Caitlin was taken aback. She'd had no idea that Brianna had thought that. But she was right. She had never felt anything more than a deep fondness for David.

'Ah, excitement and passion. Surely that fizzles out in time anyway? Isn't that why marriages fail? Once it's gone, couples are left with nothing to say to each other,' she said. But a tiny bit of her, a side she didn't care to acknowledge too often, wondered what it would be like to experience an all-consuming passion. She pushed the thought away. She was a scientist, and scientists were ruled by their heads—not their hearts.

Brianna looked at her sharply. 'Maybe you and Andrew have more in common than I thought. But, love Andrew as I do, I would advise any sane woman to keep her distance, particularly someone like you, who would have no idea how to handle a man like him.'

'Don't worry, Bri. By the sound of it, he is not my type either.' Caitlin felt a momentary stab of regret. Dismayed at her reaction, she shook her head. Good looking he may be, but her sister was right. Even if she were interested in a relationship so soon after David, the last man on earth she would be interested in would be Andrew Bedi. She didn't think men like him still existed in this day and age. She picked up a tube of sun block, keen to change the subject. 'Fancy putting some on my shoulders?'

Brianna smiled. 'Oh, Cat, I'm so glad you're here. I know I told you not to come, but now that you're here, I'm so happy.' Her voice shook slightly.

'You know I would have been here sooner if I could.' Caitlin took Brianna's cool hand in hers. 'If you hadn't convinced me not to come. Shouldn't I have believed you?'

'But I *was* fine. After all, I had Niall—and Mammy.' The two sisters shared a smile. Although they loved their mother dearly, they both agreed she could be a bit much after a while. Mrs O'Neill insisted on treating her daughters as if they were still about twelve years old and incapable of managing without her. 'I have to admit, Cat, that I was glad when she told me she had to go back home to Dad. She fussed so much, it drove me mad. She would never have agreed to go back to Ireland if you hadn't been coming out.'

Caitlin could only imagine how much her mother had fussed over Bri. Since her elder daughter had been diagnosed with breast cancer, their mother had been determined that Brianna wouldn't face her illness alone. If it weren't for the fact that her three sons were needed back home to help on the horse farm their parents owned, Caitlin was sure that their mother would have ordered her whole brood to Australia. Strapping young men though her brothers were, they were no match for Mrs O'Neill when she made up her mind about something.

'I should have come sooner, Bri,' Caitlin said softly. 'I can't believe it's been three years since we saw each other! Why on earth did we leave it so long?'

The sisters shared a look. Why *had* they left it so long? They had always been close, and when Brianna and Niall had decided to emigrate to Australia, they had promised each other that they would visit at least every couple of years. But it hadn't worked out like that. Apart from that one visit to Ireland three years ago, Brianna hadn't made it back. And Caitlin had never managed to come to Australia. Work had always got in the way.

But then, three months ago, Brianna had phoned with the devastating news that she had discovered a lump in her breast. A biopsy had confirmed their worst fears. It was cancer. Caitlin wanted to fly to her sister's side immediately, but her mother and Brianna had persuaded her to wait and apply for a sabbatical. That way her career wouldn't suffer while she was away. Indeed, having secured a post at the prestigious Brisbane hospital, there was every chance her career would be helped by her time in Australia.

Despite being pleased at the way it had worked out and delighted to be in Australia with her sister at last, Caitlin wished the circumstances had been different. She couldn't bear to think about what would happen if Brianna didn't get better. Caitlin shook her head to get rid of the negative thoughts. They all had to remain positive and believe that Brianna would make a full recovery.

'If it hadn't taken so long to arrange the work visa, I would have come as soon as I heard. Or at least been here to help you through more of the chemo.'

Brianna reached over and squeezed her hand. 'You're here now and that's what matters.' Caitlin saw the tears in her sister's eyes before she could blink them away. 'You know we have Andrew to thank for getting you the job,' Brianna continued.

'It seems that I'm in his debt quite a bit,' Caitlin said reluctantly. She hated being beholden to people.

Both women turned their gaze seaward. Niall and the children were finishing off the sandcastle. Out at sea, Caitlin caught her breath as Andrew and his board somersaulted into the air, turning over before landing and shooting along the water.

'What is he doing?' Caitlin asked, impressed. 'I've never seen anyone windsurf like that before.'

'It's called kite boarding,' Brianna replied.

'It's a bit like windsurfing, but with tricks. Andrew's very good. He's been trying to teach Niall, but it's not as easy as it looks.'

'It doesn't look easy at all,' Caitlin said as Andrew did another series of flips. 'What happens if he crashes?'

'He crashes fairly often.' Her sister laughed. 'But it doesn't put him off. He just climbs back on, and away he goes again.'

The two women watched in silence for a while.

'He says the Queensland Royal is delighted to have someone of your calibre there even for six months. It was good luck that one of the specialists wanted to spend time in the UK. I guess you'll see a fair bit of Andrew at the hospital.'

Caitlin knew she would. As a specialist obstetrician she would be working a lot with the paediatricians, of whom Andrew was one. She wondered what kind of doctor he was. An image of him lounging around flirting with the nurses and female doctors flashed across her mind. She felt unreasonably disappointed. She had no time for doctors who didn't take their work seriously. However, it was none of her business.

The sun had dried her damp skin and she slipped on her sundress. She stood, wincing slightly at the stab of pain in her calf.

'It's getting late, and everyone's bound to be getting hungry. Shall we go back to the house and make the salads?' When Caitlin had seen where her sister and her family lived she had been gobsmacked. Their house, an enormous low-slung affair, was perched on a hill just a few metres from the beach they were sitting on. It had several rooms, a hot tub and an infinity pool and views out over the sea. She had known her brother-in-law was doing well but had had no idea his fledgling business had been so successful.

'Good idea,' Brianna said, unwinding her long legs. 'I'll call Niall to start the steaks.'

'No need to disturb him,' Caitlin countered. 'We can put them on when we get back.'

'A word of warning, sis,' Brianna said, laughing. 'Men out here take their barbies seriously. Women are allowed to make the side dishes, but that's it. The cooking of the meat is a man's job.'

Caitlin laughed, then, seeing Brianna was perfectly serious, stopped. 'Fine by me. You know I hate cooking anyway. Salads are about my limit. If the men want to cook, more power to them.'

By the time the two women returned with salads and rolls, Niall and Andrew were by the fire, flipping burgers and steaks. As the smell tickled her nostrils, Caitlin realised she was starving. She had taken a couple of minutes back at the house to have a shower to rinse the sand out of her hair and off her body, and a little longer to blow-dry her hair, returning it to its smooth waves. She had tied it back in a ponytail to prevent the breeze that had whipped up from blowing it into her eyes and finally had changed into a pair of lightweight trousers and T-shirt. Impulsively, without examining her motives too closely, she applied some lip gloss in the lightest shade of pink. Putting her glasses back on, she looked at her reflection and wrinkled her nose in dissatisfaction. Not normally concerned with make-up, for the first time ever Caitlin wished she took more time and care with her appearance. *To impress Dr Bedi?* a small voice niggled at the back of her mind. Caitlin dismissed the thought immediately. Definitely not! she told herself. The important thing was that she felt and looked in control once more. Back to Dr O'Neill, obstetrician and consummate professional.

When she returned to the beach, the scent of cooking meat was drifting tantalisingly on the slight afternoon breeze. The two men seemed to be taking their cooking duties very seriously, Caitlin thought, amused as she heard them discuss whether a steak needed more marinade. Andrew had turned his wetsuit down to his hips, revealing his muscular chest. Despite herself, Caitlin felt her eyes travel over his torso, admiring the tautness of his abdomen and the defined muscles of his chest. Andrew turned, as if sensing her approving look, and caught Caitlin's eye before she could look away. He winked and she felt herself grow flustered again. Damn the man, she thought crossly.

'How's the leg?' he asked innocently.

'As you predicted, it feels a bit bruised, but otherwise fine. Thanks again. I feel such an idiot.'

'Australia can take a bit of getting used to.

I'm sure once you've been here a bit longer you'll know what's safe and what isn't. The coast here has some fantastic beaches, as you will see, but you have to be very careful about where you swim.'

Niall heaped food onto plates and everyone helped themselves to salads and buttered rolls. Niall had set up a table and chairs under the shade of an orange bougainvillea and as Caitlin ate she breathed in the tang of sea air. For the first time in months she felt energised. There was something about being here that made her realise how boring her well ordered life back in Ireland had become. As if he'd read her thoughts, Andrew turned to Caitlin.

'I understand you've been working at the Women and Children's Hospital in Dublin for the last few years. Your colleagues must think highly of you. From what I hear, it's very difficult to get accepted onto the permanent staff there. And you couldn't be more than, what—thirty?'

Caitlin flushed under his frank scrutiny. Did he think after what had happened that she was some airhead who had managed to secure her position because of who she knew rather than on her own merits? Little did he know what sacrifices she'd had to make to earn her position.

'Caitlin is being considered for a chair in obstetrics there,' Brianna said proudly. 'If she gets it, she'll be one of the youngest professors in the country.'

Catching Andrew's raised eyebrow and look of amusement, Caitlin cringed at her sister's unembarrassed boasting.

'My sister-in-law is a bit of a workaholic,' Niall added through mouthfuls of salad. 'She never stops. We've asked her to come and visit us many times since we moved here, but she's refused to take time off from work.' He smiled to show Caitlin there was no malice behind his words. He of all people knew what getting the chair in obstetrics meant to Caitlin. It seemed as if all the years of hard work were about to pay off. Not that she was there yet, but the position was within her reach. As long as she kept focussed and continued to spend her few spare hours working on publishing papers. As she thought back to her hectic life in Dublin, she appreciated for the first time just how exhausted working the hours she had, had made her. Perhaps her time here would help recharge her batteries, not that she expected an easy time of it at the Queensland Royal. Far from it. She intended to apply herself to the post here with exactly the same dedication she applied to all her jobs. At least she didn't have any research on the go at the moment. Any spare time she had here would be spent with Brianna. Of that, Caitlin was determined.

'Andrew works pretty hard too.' Brianna joined in the conversation, having returned from sorting the children out with food.

'Ah, yes, but he also plays hard,' her husband said mischievously. 'Where you get the energy is beyond me. I am far too exhausted after a day's work to do anything except read the paper and potter.'

'But you have a wife and family to keep you busy,' Andrew replied. Caitlin wasn't sure but she thought she heard a note of envy in his voice. 'Once I've finished work I'm free to do what I want.'

'Lucky devil,' Niall said, but as he smiled at his wife, Caitlin knew that he wouldn't swap what he had for the world.

By the time they had finished eating the sun was beginning to drop, turning the sky red-gold. Niall and Andrew, helped by the children, started packing up the barbecue. Caitlin sneaked a look at her sister. She looked tired. The circles under her eyes had deepened. Caitlin felt a pang of anxiety. 'Are you sure you're up to socializing, Bri?' she said. 'Shouldn't you be taking it easy? I could have waited and met Andrew when I started work. Probably would have been better anyway. God knows what impression he has of me. Not that I care,' she added hastily, catching her sister's amused look.

'I wouldn't call having Andrew over as socialising,' Brianna protested. 'He's part of the family—he's Ciaran's godfather after all.' She smiled briefly then grew serious. 'Brianna, you must listen to me. As soon as I was diagnosed, I made up my mind. I'm going to carry on as normal whenever I can. For the children's sake, if nothing else. I'm a bit tired, but as long as I rest whenever I can, I cope.' Caitlin could see the determination in the green eyes which were so like her own. 'I wouldn't have let you come at all if it hadn't been for the job. Love you as I do, the last thing I need is you fussing over me all the time like Mammy. Caitlin, I need you to support me on this and not fuss. Okay?'

'Okay,' Caitlin agreed reluctantly. 'Whatever you say. But I'm here to help whenever you need me. You just have to let me know. Promise?'

Back at the house a little later, Caitlin insisted on clearing up while Brianna went to organise the children for bed.

'I could put the children to bed if you like after I finish clearing away. You have an early night.' Catching the warning look her sister threw her, Caitlin raised her hands. 'I'm not fussing, honestly, Bri. It's just that I'm still on Irish time and suddenly wide awake. No doubt it'll hit me for six soon, but in the meantime, let me help.'

'I'm putting my children to bed,' Brianna said firmly, 'but if you want to clean the kitchen, be my guest.'

As she was stacking the dishwasher in her sister's enormous American-style kitchen, Andrew appeared, carrying some plates. Caitlin had assumed he'd left.

'Has Brianna gone to bed?' he asked, laying the dirty dishes on the granite worktop.

'She's seeing to the children,' Caitlin replied. 'Is Niall still outside?'

Andrew shook his head. 'He must be helping to put the children to bed. I should be going too.'

'How does Bri seem to you?' Caitlin asked anxiously. 'You know her well, I understand.'

Andrew looked at her sympathetically. 'She was—is—the best paediatric nurse I ever worked with. We really missed her when she stopped working to look after the kids, and then this…' He shook his head. 'But you know your sister better than I do. If anyone can beat it, she can. And I know how pleased both of them are to have you here.'

It must have been tiredness, but suddenly Caitlin felt a lump in her throat. In many ways she wished it had been her, not Brianna, who had been diagnosed. After all, it wasn't as if she had a young family depending on her. She swallowed furiously. Caitlin O'Neill did not show her emotions. Not publicly and certainly not in front of a man she barely knew and who was to be a colleague.

Andrew must have noticed. He patted her shoulder awkwardly. 'They found it early enough, you know. She's really very lucky. Everything is going to be fine.'

Caitlin wasn't convinced. But she was here and would ensure that her sister got through the next few months as painlessly as possible.

'Brianna tells me you're a paediatrician,' Caitlin said, keen to get the conversation onto neutral ground.

'Yep, for my sins,' he replied.

She flicked the kettle on. 'Would you like some coffee before you go?'

'Sure,' he said.

Caitlin looked around for where Brianna kept the mugs. Behind her Andrew reached over her to the top cupboard. For a moment she was imprisoned between him and the worktop. Acutely conscious of the heat of his body, she felt her heart begin to thud. She would have given anything to move away from him, but that would have only drawn attention to the awkwardness she felt. Thankfully, as soon as he had grabbed two mugs, he stepped away. He spooned coffee into the mugs, and then held out the jug of milk and raised one eyebrow in question.

Once their coffee was poured, Andrew sat at the kitchen table and stretched his long legs in front of him. 'Tell me about you,' he said, looking at her intently. At that moment Caitlin felt as if her world had shrunk to the kitchen and him and her. Every nerve in her body seemed to be tingling in response to him. She couldn't remember when she'd last had such an immediate reaction to a man. No, strike that. She couldn't remember *ever* having had a reaction like this to a man. It wasn't just his dark good looks, although he was pretty hot, it was the aura that surrounded him. As if he was pulling her into his magnetic field and she was powerless to resist.

'There's not much to tell,' Caitlin said, desperate for him not to see how he was affecting her. 'I am Irish—but you know that,' she said as his mouth quirked. 'I've always wanted to be a doctor, well, since about twelve anyway. I have three older brothers, whom I love but drive me mad. My mum and dad breed horses. That's about it. What about you?'

'I'm an only child.' For a moment a shadow darkened his eyes. 'My parents are from India, they're retired and live in Sydney. They came here years ago. I was born here but they're still pretty traditional. I didn't know what I wanted to do until my final year at school, but I know I made the right decision to become a doctor. I like all watersports, but am useless on a horse. Anything else you'd like to know?' He grinned at her. Caitlin wondered if he too felt the electricity that was fizzing around them.

'Hey, you started this,' Caitlin rejoined. 'The question-and-answer session, that is…' Oh, dear, what if he thought she meant something else?

Suddenly he frowned, then got to his feet. Caitlin looked up to find him towering above her. What had she said to cause the change? One minute he'd seemed relaxed, the next…as if he wanted nothing more than to get away from her as quickly as possible. A thought struck her. Did he think she was flirting with him? Did he think she had misread friendly interest for something else? She felt her toes curl with embarrassment. She stood too, feeling dwarfed by his size.

'I'll pick you up on Monday morning and take you in to the hospital if you like,' Andrew offered. 'I can give you the lowdown on the way in.'

Caitlin smiled at him gratefully. 'I'd appreciate that,' she said. 'Niall has said I'm welcome to use one of their cars whenever I need to, but I'm not sure I can find my way on the first day. I've a hopeless sense of direction. Oh, and thanks again for arranging the job for me.'

Andrew looked down at her and smiled. 'As I said, no sweat. It'll be great to have you. We're all looking forward to seeing the renowned Dr O'Neill in action. I'll see you on Monday.'

'No pressure, then,' Caitlin mouthed at his retreating back.

As Andrew pulled away from the house and headed towards the freeway that would take him home, he let out a low whistle. Dr Caitlin O'Neill was nothing like he'd imagined. He didn't know what he had expected when he'd offered to help by organising a job out for Brianna's sister. He was thinking about another doctor—a colleague—that was all. But when he had literally fished her out of the sea, he had been immediately struck by her stunning good looks. That incredible hair and those eyes! Although similar in colour to Brianna's, Caitlin's eyes had an intensity that reminded him of a cat pinning its prey. He laughed out loud at the image. Recalling the feeling of the silky-smooth skin under his fingertips, he almost groaned. This was a woman he would like in his bed. Not marriage—no, never that—but an affair. And why not? She looked like the kind of woman whose heart would be difficult to break.

CHAPTER TWO

CAITLIN dressed carefully for work on Monday. She knew that Australian hospitals were less formal than Irish ones, especially given the heat, but she wanted to create the right impression. She chose a floaty skirt that, while cool, still looked smart and teamed it with a short-sleeved white blouse. She twisted her hair into a chignon and then she was ready.

Breakfast was a far rowdier affair than Caitlin was used to. Living alone, she was used to a quiet breakfast with the paper, not this hive of activity. How could such small children make such a racket and how could Brianna think straight with all the noise?

Niall collected his briefcase and slung an overnight bag over his shoulder. He kissed his wife and sister-in-law goodbye. 'I'll be back on

Friday,' he told Brianna. 'Are you sure you'll be all right?'

'Go on, you big softy.' His wife pushed him towards the door. 'I've Caitlin here if I need anything—which I won't.' As husband and wife smiled at each other Caitlin felt a pang. What would it feel like to be loved like that? she wondered. Not that she really wanted to find out, she reminded herself. She liked her uncomplicated life back in Dublin exactly the way it was. She had work, loads of friends and plenty of hobbies to keep her busy. The last thing she needed in her life were complications, and if ever she wondered whether she was leading the right life, she just thought about her mother. Although she loved her mother fiercely, her whole life had been taken up with bringing up her large family of three boys and two girls. Caitlin had never seen her mother do anything just for herself. That wasn't the life Caitlin had mapped out for herself.

She had just finished breakfast when she heard a toot from the driveway. Looking out, she saw Andrew had arrived in a sports car. He jumped over the door and came to meet her. Unlike on

Saturday, he was dressed more formally, in a white shirt and light-coloured chinos. He looked fresh cool and very handsome. He opened the door for her with a flourish.

'Your carriage awaits,' he said.

'Why, thank you, sir,' Caitlin quipped back. 'You are too kind.'

Soon they were leaving the leafy suburbs behind and were on the freeway. As he drove, Andrew pointed out various landmarks so that Caitlin would find her way the next day. They crossed a bridge, passing modern skyscrapers. Everything seemed as different from Ireland, with its green rolling countryside and the Georgian architecture of Dublin, as it could be.

'What do you think so far?' he asked.

'Apart from the heat? I think it's wonderful,' Caitlin answered.

'It's not just the beaches, although you have to admit they are the best in the world. The Sunshine Coast is an hour to the north and the Gold Coast about the same distance south. We do some outreach work in both areas, so you'll get a chance to see them.'

'I'm looking forward to it,' Caitlin replied, gripping onto her seat as Andrew passed a car. Catching her nervous look, he laughed. 'Hey, don't worry. You're in safe hands.'

Caitlin smiled weakly in response. 'Tell me about the hospital,' she said.

By the time they had pulled up in front of the Queensland Royal, Andrew had given her a brief overview of how the medical system in Australia worked. He was a specialist paediatrician, which Caitlin already knew, and had a special interest in heart problems in neonates. The hospital was a gleaming, modern affair, all glass and stainless steel. Andrew told Caitlin that it had some of the best facilities in Australia.

As they got out of the car, an ambulance pulled up, its lights flashing. A trio of nurses was waiting at the entrance, ready to receive the casualties. Caitlin and Andrew were about to leave them to it when a nurse noticed his arrival.

'Could you hold on a minute, Dr Bedi?' she said. 'We might need you.'

Unsure where to go, Caitlin watched as the patient was unloaded. Immediately she could see that it was a woman in advanced pregnancy. From the look of distress on her face, it appeared she was in labour. Suddenly she felt her reflexes kick in. She moved towards the group, making a rapid judgement.

'Mrs Roland is in the end stage of labour,' the paramedic intoned. 'She was due to have her baby at home, but the midwife felt that labour wasn't progressing quickly enough and decided to call us. The baby's heartbeat has dropped.'

'I'm Dr O'Neill,' Caitlin introduced herself. 'One of the obstetricians. Let's get her inside so we can assess her.'

Once inside Caitlin carried out a rapid examination of the woman. It only took her a few seconds to realise that the placenta was lying in front of the baby. It was something that every obstetrician came across on a regular basis. Nevertheless, if they didn't get the baby delivered there was a chance the woman would bleed to death. In every country there were several maternal deaths every year due to the condition. There was no time to lose. Every second counted if they were to save the woman and her unborn child. 'Placenta praevia,' she said. 'She needs to go to Theatre immediately.'

'I'll tell Theatre to expect us,' one of the nurses said, turning towards the phone.

'I'll scrub in too,' Andrew said. Even if they managed to get the baby delivered safely there was every chance it might need resuscitating. 'C'mon, Caitlin, let's go.'

Caitlin struggled to keep up with his long strides as they rushed towards Theatre. A nurse handed her some scrubs and clogs and she scrubbed up beside Andrew, mentally counting off the minutes.

'Right in at the deep end,' Andrew said sympathetically. 'We didn't even manage to get you up to the ward.'

By the time they were scrubbed and gowned, Mrs Roland had been anesthetised and was lying prepped on the theatre table.

Caitlin cut into the abdomen from left to right just above the pubic bone. As the skin separated, she made another incision into the uterus, careful not to damage the precious contents. As she pulled the baby out, she glanced at the clock.

Ten minutes had passed since the patient had arrived at the hospital. She was pleased to see none of her speed had deserted her.

The baby, a little boy, was slightly floppy and blue. Caitlin handed him to the midwife, who rushed the baby across to the resuscitator.

'He's a bit flat,' the midwife called out. As Caitlin started to close she was aware of the tension in the room. Andrew needed to get oxygen into the baby, and soon. Across the woman's abdomen she watched as he tipped the baby's head back gently before slipping in a paediatric endotracheal tube, feeling his way through the larynx and into the lungs. Then he attached an ambu-bag and started feeding oxygen into the tiny lungs. Every movement he made was calm and assured, and this fed into the atmosphere of the theatre. There was no panic. Everyone was simply going about their jobs quietly and efficiently. Caitlin was impressed. She guessed the team had worked together many times before.'

'Heart rate 140 and he's a good colour now,' Andrew announced to the room to a collective sigh of relief. 'I think baby is going to be fine. We'll get them up to Special Care, but I think we should be able to reunite mother and baby quite soon.'

'Maybe not tonight,' Caitlin said. 'I'll want to keep an eye on her in the labour ward overnight, in case of post-partum haemorrhage.'

While the baby was being taken away to the special care nursery, accompanied by the paediatric nurse and Andrew, Caitlin finished closing the wound. She felt a trickle of perspiration run down her forehead and was grateful when one of the nurses wiped it away. Once Mrs Roland had woken from the anaesthetic, she would see her and let her know what was happening. She was pleased that her first case had gone well—not that she doubted her ability, but Caitlin knew that sometimes even straightforward cases could suddenly go wrong.

After she had finished in Theatre, she asked one of the nurses to take her to Special Care. She wanted to check on the baby before she spoke to the mother.

She found Andrew bending over the infant,

listening to its chest. He looked up at her, his deep brown eyes warm. 'He's going to be fine, I think,' he said. 'We'll know better in a few days. You did a good job back there.'

Caitlin looked around the small high-tech unit. It reminded her of the one back in Dublin, but she guessed that there was a uniformity with all hospitals in the Western world. There were five babies in at the moment, with anxious parents sitting by their incubators. Her heart went out to them. It must be so hard to feel so helpless, to know that the life of your child depended on the doctors and nurses.

Having finished examining the baby she had recently delivered, and announcing himself satisfied for the time being, Andrew suggested he show her around.

'We have around four thousand deliveries a year here,' he said. 'We get difficult cases from quite far away. The air ambulance brings mothers and kids in on a regular basis. You might like to go out with the team some time.'

'I'd love to,' Caitlin said enthusiastically. 'I've

never been on anything like it before. I guess in a country of this size, it happens a lot.'

'Often enough,' Andrew said. 'We take turns being on call for the air ambulance. I'll rota you in for the same time as me. Okay?'

At Caitlin's nod he went on. 'I'll take you up to Personnel. I know you sent all your paperwork in advance, but there may be one or two pieces they need from you. After that I'll give you the tour.'

After she'd completed the necessary paperwork, Andrew introduced her to the midwives and doctors she'd be working with. There were too many faces for her to remember everyone's names straight away, that would take time, but all the staff seemed very welcoming.

Her first afternoon was to be spent in Theatre. One of the senior midwives, a cheerful woman called Linda, took her on a round of the antenatal ward. Andrew left them to it while he went to do his own rounds. After the ward round Linda took Caitlin to the general gynaecology ward and introduced her to the patients she had scheduled for Theatre.

After seeing all the patients on her afternoon's list, Linda stopped in front of a woman who was perched on the end of the bed and looked as if she was ready to run a mile.

'This is Mrs Mary Oliphant,' Linda introduced the woman. 'She's in to have her tubes examined. She and her husband have been trying for a baby for a year, and their family doctor thinks she should have her tubes checked before they think about IVF.'

'Good idea,' Caitlin said. Mrs Oliphant seemed to relax a little. 'It's a very quick procedure,' Caitlin said. 'We'll take you down to the scanning room and pass a catheter through your cervix, squirt some dye and have a look. We don't even need to anaesthetise you, but we'll give you a couple of painkillers as it can be uncomfortable. The good news is that you'll have the results straight away.'

'And if my tubes are blocked? What then? Does that mean we won't be able to have children?' Mary's lip trembled. 'We really want a baby.' A tear slipped down her cheek. 'I blame myself. I was determined to wait until my career was established before we started a family. But what if I've left it too late?'

'Hey, let's not get ahead of ourselves,' Caitlin said soothingly. 'Let's do the echovist first and we can talk again then.' She took her hand. 'Anyway, you're not that old.' She smiled. 'Although a woman's fertility does decline markedly after the age of thirty-five, you're still on the right side of forty. And there is a test we can do which will tell us just how well your ovaries are responding. I'll take a blood sample today, and I should have the results for you soon. I also suggest that we test your husband. That way, if you need to think about IVF you'll be ready to go. How does that sound?'

As she spoke a thought slipped into her head. Time was passing for her too. It was quite possible that if she changed her mind about wanting children, she too would find she'd left it too late. It was one thing not to want children, quite another to have the choice taken away. She squeezed the thought to the back of her mind. Why was she suddenly thinking children might be an option in the future, when until now she had been sure children weren't for her? She forced her attention back to her patient. It was Mary who she had to think about. She deserved her full attention.

Mary smiled, seeming reassured. 'That sounds great,' she said. 'I just want to know so we can decide our next step. Thank you for taking the trouble to talk to me.'

'Hey, that's what we're here for.' Caitlin smiled. 'I'll see you down in the scanning room shortly. First let's take that blood sample.'

Quickly, Caitlin took a sample of blood from Mrs Oliphant's arm and passed it to Linda.

As they moved away Linda said, 'There's one more lady I'd like you to see. I've already spoken to Dr Bedi about her, and he's interested to know what you think.' Curious, Caitlin let herself be led across into one of the single rooms. Sitting up in bed, reading a magazine listlessly, was the patient Linda had asked her to see.

'This is Mrs Levy,' Linda said, passing her chart to Caitlin. 'As you can see, she's twenty-nine weeks pregnant. She was admitted earlier today with an elevated blood pressure of

160 over 100, plus protein in her urine. In her first pregnancy she had to be delivered prematurely because of high blood pressure.'

Caitlin had seen the condition often. It was always a difficult judgement call. On the one hand, there was no treatment and the only sure way of preventing the condition from getting worse was to deliver the baby. However, Mrs Levy was only twenty-eight weeks pregnant and although Caitlin knew that the hospital had the necessary equipment to look after a pre-term baby, there was always a chance that the baby would suffer brain damage or even worse if it was delivered so early.

'What does Dr Bedi think?' she asked Linda as they moved away from the patient.

'He'd prefer us to wait and monitor her closely over the next few days.'

It wasn't an unreasonable decision, Caitlin knew. Every day the baby stayed safely in the mother's womb increased its chances of survival.

'Could we arrange to have Mrs Levy scanned?' Caitlin asked, making up her mind. 'I'll do it myself before Theatre.' She went back to her patient.

'You're probably well aware of our concerns, Mrs Levy. I'm sure they have been discussed with you.'

'Please call me Patricia. Mrs Levy always makes me think of my mother-in-law.' She smiled, before the anxious look returned to her eyes. 'That nice Dr Bedi came to see me and explained everything.'

Did he, now? Caitlin thought, wishing that he had spoken to her before discussing options with the patient. She decided to wait until she had spoken to him and had the scan results before speaking to Patricia again. 'I'd like to scan you as soon as we can get a scanner up here,' she told the patient. 'I'll see you in a little while, okay? Then we can decide on the best way forward.'

Patricia clutched Caitlin's hand. 'I really want this baby,' she said. 'They told me it's a girl and as I have two boys, it will make my family complete.'

Caitlin patted her hand reassuringly. 'We'll do our best for you, I promise. In the meantime, the best thing you can do for your baby is try and relax.'

After rounds Linda took Caitlin into the staff-room for a cup of coffee. 'What do you think so far?' she asked as she poured them mugs from the pot that had been made earlier.

'I'm impressed,' Caitlin admitted. 'The facilities, at least what I've seen so far, are impressive.'

'I hear from the others that you know Dr Bedi. He's lovely, don't you think?'

Caitlin wasn't quite sure how to answer. What was she supposed to say to that? That, yes, he was gorgeous and that she fancied the pants off him? 'He seems very nice,' she said noncommittally.

'Half the nurses and doctors here are in love with him. The other half are married.' Linda laughed. 'Thank goodness I'm in the second half. Otherwise I'd be doomed to have my heart broken, like the rest.'

Caitlin wasn't used to such frankness and wasn't sure how to respond. Thankfully, as she was searching frantically for a more neutral subject, Andrew himself appeared.

'They told me I'd find you here,' he said, pouring himself a glass of water from the cooler and gulping it greedily. 'I wondered if you wanted to see the paeds wards before we have lunch. Your theatre list starts at 1.30. Right?' She eyed him, mentally readjusting her opinion of him in light of what Linda had told her.

Caitlin stood. 'I'd love to see the children's ward,' she said. 'And meet the staff.' She finished her coffee and rinsed her cup. 'Thanks, Linda,' she said as she followed Andrew out of the staffroom. 'I'll see you after Theatre.'

She followed Andrew out of the staffroom.

'I don't think we should leave Mrs Levy any longer,' she said. 'She's showing all the signs of pre-eclampsia—raised blood pressure and protein in her urine. If we don't deliver her and her condition gets worse then there is a chance she'll start fitting and we'll lose her. I'm sure neither of us want to be faced with a maternal death.'

Andrew turned and looked at her. 'The last two scans place her at twenty-eight weeks,' he said. 'There's not been much growth since then.' He frowned. Caitlin wondered if he was unused to having his opinion challenged. Underneath his easygoing exterior she thought there was a man who, once he had made up his mind, was loath to change it. It was clear in the way the staff acquiesced to him that he was used to being deferred to. On the other hand, so was she. She trusted her instinct, and if she were back in Ireland nobody would have questioned her decision.

'If we deliver her now, then there is a chance the baby won't survive,' he continued. 'Even another couple of days would give it a better chance.'

Caitlin held her ground. 'If we wait another couple of days and the mother develops full-blown eclampsia then there's a good chance that we'll lose the baby as well as the mother. Is that a risk you're prepared to take? Because I'm not sure I am.'

They stared at each other, neither willing to give an inch.

'We should go and speak to the patient at least,' Caitlin said eventually. 'We should give her all the facts and let her decide.'

'Do you think that's fair?' Andrew countered. 'If she decides to go ahead and let us deliver the baby, and the baby dies, she'll carry that burden always. She'll always wonder if she made the right decision.'

'And if she takes your advice and waits, and she and the baby both die, then what about the rest of her family? She has two children under the age of five. Do you think it's fair to leave them without a mother?' Caitlin felt her voice catch on the last words as an image of her niece and nephew growing up without their mother flashed across her mind.

Andrew looked at her sharply. 'Are you sure this isn't becoming personal, Caitlin?' he asked softly.

Caitlin gritted her teeth in frustration. She never let her personal feelings or emotions interfere with her professional judgement. But that didn't mean that she looked on her patients just as obstetric dilemmas—she prided herself on taking all aspects of their lives into account when making a clinical decision. How dared he suggest otherwise? Even if he already thought of her as some sort of pathetic female that needed rescuing. Now he was accusing her of being over-emotional and letting her worry about her sister cloud her judgement. Well, she would soon put him right.

'Let me make one thing absolutely clear, Dr Bedi. It's important we understand one another if we are going to be making joint decisions about patients.' Her voice was cold and clipped, even to her own ears, but she made no attempt to soften her tone. 'The decisions I make are *always*—' she emphasised the last word '—made on the basis of what is good for my patient. I never let personal feelings cloud my judgement.' Aware that she had curled her hands into fists, she made herself relax. What was it about this man which caused her to have such strong reactions?

'I'm glad to hear it, Dr O'Neill,' he said calmly. 'Because if I ever had reason to think you weren't up to the job, believe you me, regardless of the friendship I have with your family. I wouldn't hesitate to have you removed from the case. Now, do *I* make myself clear?'

CHAPTER THREE

STUNNED, Caitlin could only stare openmouthed at Andrew.

'Well, now that we understand each other,' she said stiffly, 'shall we continue?' She marched off in what she hoped was the general direction of Paediatrics, not caring whether Andrew was following or not. Of all the insufferable, conceited, big-headed... She was fuming to herself when Andrew caught her arm and stopped her in her tracks.

She glared at him, before seeing the look of apology in his deep brown eyes.

'I'm sorry,' he said, 'that was unforgivable of me.'

'Yes, it was,' Caitlin said. Then she softened at his look of genuine remorse. 'Do you really have doubts about my clinical judgement?' she asked, puzzled. 'I know you had me checked out thoroughly before you arranged the job for me.'

'I did,' Andrew said. 'And I don't have doubts. It's just…' He hesitated. 'Let's just say that I have my reasons.'

'Shouldn't you tell me what they are?' Caitlin said.

'There's no need. I agree we should wait for the scan results before we decide what to do. Okay?'

Caitlin was tempted to press further, but she could tell from the set of his chin that she was unlikely to get anything more from Andrew. But she was a patient woman. Whatever it was, she would find out soon enough.

'Okay,' Caitlin said. 'Now, let's go and see this paediatric ward of yours.'

After a quick tour of the children's ward, Caitlin left Andrew checking his patients and made her way to the scanning room where Mrs Oliphant was waiting for her.

'Hey, how are you doing?' Caitlin said. Mary just smiled weakly.

Caitlin passed the catheter then turned the

monitor towards her patient and pointed to the screen.

'Look,' she told the anxious woman. 'You can see both the ovaries. That's the left one and there's the right. And see that little blob there? That's a follicle with an egg developing inside. So far so good. Everything is normal.' She withdrew the catheter. 'You can get dressed now.'

Once Mrs Oliphant was dressed and sitting down, Caitlin turned to her. 'I've also had the blood results back. And they're consistent with the scan we've just done. Your ovaries are looking good. And the embryologists have told me that Richard's results are also normal. So I'm going to suggest that you go home and keep trying for another six months. If you're still not pregnant by then, we'll talk about IVF. But I've got a feeling that you won't need it.'

Mary relaxed and smiled broadly. 'It's such a relief to know,' she said. 'I can't tell you how worried I've been.'

'Sometimes,' Caitlin said gently, 'I find that once couples relax, nature just takes it course. And if it doesn't, well, you can come and see me again. But for now I want you and Richard to go home and have plenty of sex.'

She saw a happy and relieved Mary out, and then asked whether the scanner could be taken to the antenatal ward for Mrs Levy's scan.

Once back on the antenatal ward, Caitlin prepped Patricia's abdomen with gel, apologising for the cold sensation. Then she placed the wand over her abdomen and turned the screen towards the patient so that she was able to see what Caitlin was seeing.

'See that over there.' She pointed to the heart. 'That's the baby's heart. As you can see, it's beating strongly.' Patricia looked entranced as Caitlin proceeded to point out arms and legs. The image was so good that she was even able to show Mrs Levy her baby sucking her thumb. 'And as you've been told already, she is a healthy little girl. I put her at about twenty-eight weeks and three days.'

Mrs Levy lay back on the bed, looking thoughtful. 'It makes it seem more real, seeing her there on the screen.' She closed her eyes and Caitlin watched as tears slid out from underneath her eyelids. 'I just don't know what to do for the best. If only my Jack was here to help me decide.' Caitlin knew from the notes that Mrs Levy's husband had been killed in a traffic accident early on in the pregnancy. Her heart went out to the distraught woman. 'My other two, my boys, they are my first husband's,' she went on. 'We divorced when my youngest was two. I thought that was me. That it would just be me and the boys. And then Jack came along, and that was that. We fell in love and married a few months later.' She opened her eyes and Caitlin could see the memories brighten her eyes.

Caitlin perched beside her patient on the bed. 'Go on,' she said softly.

'As I say, we got married, once the children had got to know him, and then started trying for a baby. It took a couple of years for me to get pregnant, you know. I was getting close to forty by this time.' She paused, her eyes misting over. 'He was so excited, he didn't have children of his own, never having married before. He was just like a little kid himself. He even went out and bought a crib the day after I took the pregnancy test.'

Caitlin was aware of somebody coming to stand behind her. She glanced over her shoulder to see Andrew. Patricia went on.

'Then just a couple of months later he was dead.' She started to cry in earnest. Wordlessly, Andrew passed her some tissues and they waited in silence while she fought for control. Eventually, she blew her nose.

'So, you see,' she said once her sobs had subsided, 'I can't risk losing this baby. It's all I have left of Jack.' She looked from Andrew to Caitlin, her eyes begging them to understand. 'Dr Bedi knows all this,' she said quietly. 'That's why he said we might be able to risk waiting a day or two.'

'But,' Caitlin said gently, 'you do realise if we wait too long there's a risk you could develop full-blown eclampsia and might die. What about your other children? They'd be left without a mother.'

'I don't want to die,' Patricia said fiercely. 'I don't want to leave my kids, but Dr Bedi says you'll watch me carefully.'

'Okay,' Caitlin agreed reluctantly. 'We'll watch and wait. But I'm warning you, if there is the slightest sign of your condition worsening, I'm getting you delivered. Agreed?' She looked at Andrew for confirmation and was relieved when he nodded.

'I'll ask them to call me at home if there's any change,' he said.

'As will I,' Caitlin added. 'I'll do the section myself.'

'I'd feel so much better if you'll both be there,' Mrs Levy said, hope brightening her eyes.

'But they might have to go ahead and deliver you if I can't get here in time,' Caitlin warned.

'I understand,' Patricia said. 'Thank you both for taking care of me and listening.'

Andrew and Caitlin left Patricia to get some rest. A glance at her watch told Caitlin that she was due in Theatre.

'Did you know all that?' she asked. 'Is that the reason you wanted to wait?'

'Partly,' Andrew said. 'At the end of the day I want the same thing you do. A healthy baby and a mother who survives to look after it. But,' he said, 'I don't think we should ever look at patients as if they were simply their medical problems. We need to see them as people, all with different needs requiring different solutions.' Caitlin bristled. Was he suggesting that she didn't see her patients as individuals? He had no right to make that assessment of her. But, she admitted to herself, was there just the tiniest bit of truth in it? Was that why she was so drawn to the academic side of her chosen speciality? Because it was easier than dealing with real people and real emotions? He grinned down at her, and Caitlin's heart gave a curious flip. 'You and I are on the same side after all.'

Caitlin's surgeries were straightforward and she didn't see Andrew again until it was time to leave for the day. She felt wrung out, the perspiration trickling down her shoulder blades. Before she left she checked on Mrs Levy. There was no change in her condition. Caitlin asked that the staff be asked to call her should her condition change during the night. When she checked her watch it was after six. It had been a long first day. Suddenly anxious to get home to check on Brianna, she paged Andrew and told him she'd meet him by the hospital entrance. When he finally arrived he was whistling cheerfully.

'Hey,' he said. 'Ready to go?'

As they set off home, the sun was sinking in the sky. Caitlin welcomed the breeze as they made their way through the traffic. She was uncomfortably aware of Andrew in the small space of his sports car. She could smell the faint tang of his aftershave and was conscious of his long fingers as he steered the car through the traffic. What would it be like to feel those fingers on her skin? she wondered. Immediately she was horrified at the direction her thoughts were taking. What was wrong with her? Thinking like this was so unlike her. Maybe the strangeness of a new country was affecting her? It wasn't as if she had the time or inclination for romance. Not with so much on her plate and certainly not with this man.

'I gather you looked in on Mrs Levy,' he said as they reached the edge of the suburb where Brianna lived.

'Yes, before I paged you,' she said. 'All her

results are exactly the same as before. So perhaps we made the right decision to wait. I hope so.'

'Mmm. I went to see her too. If her condition changes, they'll call me. Believe me, I'm as determined as you that both will pull through,' he said, his mouth set in a grim line.

They turned into the drive of Brianna's house, sending a flock of rainbow lorikeets into the air. 'They are so beautiful,' Caitlin said, admiring the vividly coloured birds with their bright red beaks and green wings. 'Just like something I'd expect to find in the Amazon rainforest.'

'They're all over Brisbane,' Andrew replied. He looked at her thoughtfully. 'If you're interested in seeing more of the same, as well as experiencing a rainforest, you don't have to go as far as the Amazon. There's a place not far out of Brisbane in the Green Mountains called O'Reilly's.' He grinned at her. 'No relation, I presume?' Not waiting for a reply, he continued, 'I go up there on a regular basis. It's a great way to escape the heat of the city and there are amazing walks in the rainforest. They even have one that takes you right across the treetops.'

'It sounds wonderful,' Caitlin agreed. 'But I'm not really here to amuse myself. When I'm not working, I'd rather spend the time with Brianna.'

'You could go together,' Andrew suggested. 'I believe there's plenty to keep the kids busy. And if you're interested, there's also my house up the coast. Niall and the family often stay there. You're welcome to use it too while you're here.'

'That's very generous of you,' Caitlin said. 'Are you coming in?' she asked, levering herself out of the car.

'No, thanks,' he said. 'You'll want to spend time alone with Brianna, after being away all day. I'll leave you to it.' And with a spurt of gravel he had gone. Caitlin stared after his departing car. He was a mass of contradictions. One minute a flirtatious playboy, the next a kind and sensitive friend. She didn't quite know what to make of him. All she knew was that Dr Andrew Bedi was having a very unsettling effect on her and that was the last thing she wanted or needed right now.

'How did your first day go?' Brianna asked. Caitlin had helped organise the children for bed and the two women were relaxing in the kitchen with some iced tea.

'It was interesting,' Caitlin said slowly. 'But nothing very different from back home. How was your day?' She searched her sister's face for signs of tiredness. Although the tumour had been large enough to be classed as Stage II, the positioning of it meant that Brianna had been able to have a lumpectomy rather than a mastectomy. While the surgery had been straightforward, Caitlin could see that the follow-up chemotherapy was taking its toll on her sister. Thankfully she only had one more session to complete. Then the doctors would wait a month, giving her body some time to recover, before starting Brianna on a course of radiotherapy.

'I feel good, you know,' Brianna said softly. 'The effects of the chemo weren't nearly as bad as I was expecting. Except perhaps for the loss of my hair.' She ruefully touched the scarf she was using to cover her scalp. 'Losing my eyelashes, believe it or not, was almost the worst part of this whole business.'

Caitlin reached over and hugged her sister.

'Were you frightened? Silly question—you must have been.'

'I never once believed that I wouldn't get better. When you have two small children, you have to believe that.'

Brianna swivelled round in her seat and looked at Caitlin. 'What about you, Cat? Have you thought about what this might mean for you?'

Caitlin frowned. 'I'm not sure I know what you mean.'

'C'mon, sis, you're a doctor. Aunty Molly died of breast cancer when she was thirty-six. And now I have it at thirty-two. It's likely there is a genetic component. Don't tell me it hasn't crossed your mind.'

It hadn't. When Caitlin had first heard about Brianna she had been too caught up worrying about her to even consider what it might mean for her. Then there had been the arrangements for her job to think about. But now she thought about it, she realised Brianna was right. There was a strong possibility she might develop breast cancer herself.

'I'll go see someone,' she said. 'Perhaps

arrange for a mammogram. But I do check myself regularly, and so far I don't think there's anything to worry about.'

'I think about Siobhan,' Brianna admitted. 'Her chances of getting breast cancer are also increased.' She took a sip of her drink, looking more worried than Caitlin had seen her before. 'You hear about girls having a double mastectomy because they're so worried. How on earth will I advise her when she's older?'

Caitlin's thoughts were whirling around inside her head. This was something she just hadn't thought about. Although she had tried to reassure Brianna, she knew that what she was saying was true. Both she and Siobhan did have an increased chance of getting the disease. And if she ever had a daughter, she too would be at risk. Would she be prepared to take that chance? But she and Brianna were getting way ahead of themselves.

'You know, by the time Siobhan is older, they might well have found a cure. Detection is getting so much better now, as are survival rates. They've come a long way since Aunt Molly's time.'

'I heard somewhere that there is a test that can tell you whether you have the gene,' Brianna said thoughtfully. 'Do you think we can find out about it?'

'Of course,' Caitlin said. 'Leave it to me.' She squeezed her sister's hand, trying to inject all the reassurance she could into the touch.

'I know you are going to be just fine. You'll get through this and I'll be here to make sure you do.'

'Is that the sister or the doctor speaking?' Brianna asked with a small smile.

'Both,' said Caitlin firmly. 'Now, don't you think it's time for bed?'

It felt to Caitlin as if she had only been asleep for a couple of minutes when she was woken by her mobile phone. Switching on the bedside light, she squinted at the unfamiliar number on her phone.

'Hello. Dr O'Neill?' said the voice. 'It's the hospital here. We spoke to Dr Bedi and he said to call you. I hope you don't mind.'

Instantly Caitlin was wide awake. 'What is it?' she asked. 'Is it Mrs Levy?'

'Yes,' the voice replied. 'Her blood pressure

has risen, causing some concern. Dr Bedi is on his way in, in case we have to section her. He said that you might want to perform the procedure.'

'I'll be there as soon as I can.'

Twenty minutes later Caitlin was at the hospital. At four in the morning the roads were clear of traffic, and she was relieved that she remembered the way, only taking one wrong turn.

She rushed up to the antenatal ward and found Andrew already there in discussion with the midwives. Mrs Levy was looking anxiously from one to the other. She seemed even more worried when she spotted Caitlin.

'I guess that means you've made up your minds to deliver me,' she said despondently, sinking back in her pillows.

'Not necessarily,' Caitlin said softly. 'I need to have a chat with Dr Bedi before we decide.' She looked at the chart, which Andrew had passed over. She could see from the notes the night staff had made that Patricia's platelets had dropped and that she was showing the first signs of renal failure.

'I don't think we can wait any longer,' she

said. Andrew nodded his agreement. 'I'll let Theatre know,' he said, turning away.

Caitlin returned to Patricia's bedside. 'I'm sorry, Patricia, but we can't wait any longer. We have to get you delivered, and Dr Bedi agrees.'

Patricia squeezed her eyes shut, but not before Caitlin could see that they were awash with tears. 'Please,' she whispered. 'Can't we wait? Just a little longer. It's too soon.'

Caitlin shook her head. 'It's too dangerous,' she said. 'But Dr Bedi will do everything he can to save your baby. You just have to trust us now.'

Suddenly Patricia sat up in bed, panic-stricken. 'I can't see!' she cried out. 'What's happening? Please, someone, help me!'

Caitlin whirled round, her heart sinking. Loss of eyesight was a clear symptom that Patricia's condition had worsened. Now they really needed to get her delivered. Time was against them.

'It's okay, Patricia,' she said. 'It's probably only temporary. As soon as we get you delivered, everything will be okay.' But even as she said the words she wondered if they were true. There was every chance they could lose her and the baby.

She glanced across at Andrew and could see that the same thoughts had crossed his mind.

'Let's get her down to Theatre—now! Page the anaesthetist to tell whoever it is to meet us in Theatre,' Andrew said, unlocking the wheels of the bed. Helped by Caitlin and the midwives, they pushed the bed towards Theatre.

Caitlin's heart was pounding as they ran with Patricia. Once there, she still had to scrub up. That would take five minutes, but would give the anaesthetist time to put Patricia under. How quickly they would get the baby out would depend on how quickly she could carry out the procedure. At this point, every second counted.

Leaving Patricia in the care of the theatre staff, Caitlin scrubbed up alongside Andrew.

'It seems you were right after all,' Andrew said grimly. 'I really hoped we had some more time.'

'It was the right decision to wait,' Caitlin said. 'I'll get the baby out, and then it's up to you.'

By the time they had finished scrubbing up, Patricia had been anesthetised and Caitlin wasted no time in cutting open her abdomen. Instead of the transverse incision, which left a neater scar, she went for a longitudinal cut which would allow her to get the baby out quicker. Now was not the time to think about cosmetics. It only took her three minutes from the first incision to removing the baby from its protective sac. A record even for her. She passed the tiny baby, not much bigger than her hand, across to Andrew, who was standing by with a nurse from the special care unit ready to resuscitate the baby. The tiny girl was so small Caitlin could see every vein through its translucent skin.

'C'mon, darling,' Caitlin whispered as she passed the baby across. 'Fight. Your mummy needs you.'

Caitlin could have heard a pin drop as everyone held their breath, hardly daring to hope. She forced her attention away from what was happening behind her to her patient. Although the baby was out, the mother wasn't out of danger yet. She needed to deliver the placenta and close the wound. Only after that could she be sure Patricia would make it. Behind her she was aware of voices and movement. Eventually, just as she had finished closing, Andrew called out.

'We're taking her up to Intensive Care.' And then with a last flutter of activity they were gone.

Thankfully, Patricia's blood pressure dropped dramatically now that the baby had been delivered. Caitlin waited with her until she came round from the anaesthetic, desperately worried that the loss of eyesight might be permanent. It was so unfair. Patricia already had had more than her fair share of tragedy. What if she were left blind and her baby died or was left brain damaged? It would be too cruel.

But eventually Patricia's eyes flickered open. Caitlin held her breath as Patricia slowly focussed on her face.

'Dr O'Neill,' Patricia said. 'How's my baby?'

Caitlin sighed with relief. Patricia's blindness had been temporary. Thank God they had got her to Theatre in time. Now all they needed to do was to ensure her baby survived.

'She's holding her own,' Caitlin said softly. 'Now that you're awake, I'll go and see her myself and report back.'

Patricia struggled to sit up, her face twisted in pain. 'I want to see my baby,' she cried. 'I need to see her and she needs me!' Gently, Caitlin eased her back down. 'I will take you to see her as soon as it's possible. I promise. And I'll come straight back down and tell you everything once I've seen her. In the meantime, promise me you'll take it easy?'

Patricia closed her eyes, defeated, sinking back into the peace of sleep. 'Be as quick as you can,' she whispered. 'Tell them I need my little girl.'

After she'd left Patricia, Caitlin went to the special care unit. Andrew and the team were still working on the baby. Caitlin stood to the side and watched, not wanting to get in the way. Eventually Andrew stood back from the incubator and peeled off his gloves.

'Right, keep a close eye on her. But well done, everyone. The next twenty-four hours are crucial.' Then he noticed Caitlin and walked across to her. She could see the fatigue in his eyes, but he was smiling. Caitlin's heart leapt. It was a good sign.

'Baby's breathing,' he said softly. 'It's still touch and go and will be for the next few days, even weeks, but she has a chance. How's Mum?'

'She's going to be fine,' Caitlin answered. 'Her eyesight has returned.' She saw the look of relief in Andrew's eyes. 'She'll want to see her baby once she's fully recovered from the anaesthesia. In the meantime, I've promised to report back on how her baby is doing.' She walked across to the incubator and looked at the tiny form that was almost obscured by tubes and lines. Although she had seen babies in such a condition before, she never found it any easier. She knew Patricia would have to be prepared for seeing her baby like this.

'Does she have a chance?' she asked.

'I think so,' Andrew said. 'We will do everything we possibly can.' He straightened his shoulders. 'But, there's nothing more I can do for the time being—the nurses have everything under control. I'll check up on her once I've spoken to Patricia.'

'The nurses will page me as soon as she comes round properly,' Caitlin said. 'We can both speak to her then.'

'Coffee?' Andrew asked.

'I'd love some.'

Caitlin followed him into the staffroom just off the main ward. As always after an emergency, Caitlin felt the adrenaline drain away, leaving her feeling emotionally as well as physically exhausted. She accepted a coffee gratefully.

'Are you okay?' Andrew asked. Despite her best intentions, it seemed as if he were able to see through the exterior she tried so hard to present to the outside world. His dark brown eyes seemed to drill right through her. But as she returned his gaze, she could tell he was equally affected by the drama.

'She looks so small and defenceless,' she said. 'It's hard to imagine that someone that tiny can survive.'

'Every day more and more babies survive, you know that,' Andrew said gently. 'Her chances were helped by you getting her out so quickly.'

'But even if she survives, we both know she might have brain damage.'

'Yes,' Andrew agreed. 'On the other hand, she could be perfectly all right. That's what we have to hope for. We have to stay positive.'

'How can you do it, day after day?' Caitlin

asked. 'You must lose so many children. At least in my specialty, the outcome is usually positive.'

'And increasingly so in mine,' Andrew said. 'The trick, I find, is not to get too emotionally involved.'

'Like me, you mean?' Caitlin said, her temper rising. 'Well, I'm sorry, Mr Cool, that we can't all be machines.'

Andrew placed his mug on the counter and stepped towards her until he was towering over her. His dark eyes glinted dangerously. 'Is that how you see me?' he asked. 'As a machine?' He raised his hand and traced a finger across her cheekbone. Caitlin felt herself tingle. 'I can assure you, Dr O'Neill, that I am no machine.'

Caitlin was rooted to the spot. She felt her breath catch in her throat. She could feel the heat of his body radiating into hers. Then he dropped his hand and turned away from her. Caitlin felt her knees wobble and had to hold on to the worktop to hold herself upright. What was this man doing to her? Why was he having this effect on her? He might be good looking, but he was not her type. Far too masculine and assured of his own sexuality. Caitlin had an image of him flinging her across his shoulder before marching off to some cave. The image made her smile. Just then one of the midwives popped her head in. She stood for a moment, glancing from Andrew to Caitlin, looking puzzled, and Caitlin wondered if she could sense the sexual tension in the room.

'The ward called, Dr O'Neill. They thought you'd be here. Mrs Levy has come round. They said you wanted to know.'

'Thank you,' Caitlin replied. She rinsed her cup in the sink. 'Shall we go, Dr Bedi?'

CHAPTER FOUR

CAITLIN didn't see much of Andrew over the next few days. She went up to SCBU a couple of times a day to check on baby Levy's progress and would sometimes catch sight of Andrew examining a patient or in discussion with the nursing staff. Every time she caught a glimpse of his dark head, she was uncomfortably aware of the effect on her heart rate.

Patricia was always by her baby's cot, willing her on. 'I'm so desperate to hold her,' she told Caitlin. 'I just feel that if I could hold her in my arms, if she could feel me, know that I'm here…' Her voice broke. 'That her mummy is right here beside her…I would feel so much better. All I've been able to do is touch her finger.'

'Just hang in there,' Caitlin said. 'She's getting stronger every day. And she'll recognise your voice. The nurses tell me you talk to her all the time.'

'And sing,' Patricia said. 'Although my voice isn't up to much.' She managed a wry smile. Caitlin glanced around the room. All the incubators had mothers and in some cases fathers by the cots. All wore the same anxious expressions.

'How are your other children?' Caitlin asked.

'My mother has come to stay with them. Thank goodness she was prepared to move out of her house and into mine. But I miss them so much. They come to see me, but it's not the same as being with them all the time. I've never been away from them before. Not even overnight.' Then she started crying again. 'I wish Jack was here. It's not fair. He should be here with me.'

Caitlin felt helpless to comfort the distraught woman. It was so unfair the way life dealt the cards sometimes. She became aware that Andrew was standing behind her. He crouched down beside the stricken woman.

'Hey,' he said softly. 'What's this? Your baby is making progress. She's a fighter. Just like her mother, I suspect.'

'Patricia needs to hold her baby,' Caitlin said.

'I think we can arrange that.' Very gently he reached inside the incubator and lifted the infant out, careful not to disturb any of the lines. In his large hands the baby looked even smaller, more defenceless, if that were possible. Seeing what he was doing, one of the nursing staff came rushing over.

'Dr Bedi, what do you think you're doing? The baby needs to stay in the incubator.'

'What this baby needs, more than any medicine we can provide, is to feel her mother's arms,' he said firmly, before placing his delicate bundle in Patricia's arms. 'Only for a few moments,' he said, smiling down at her.

Caitlin felt a lump in her throat as she watched Patricia gaze down at her baby.

'Hello there,' Patricia said softly, her voice little more than a whisper. 'Hello, my darling girl. This is Mummy speaking.' Caitlin had to turn away as tears pricked her eyes. Impatiently she blinked them away. She was damned if she was going to let anyone see the ultra-cool Dr O'Neill with her defences down. But catching Andrew's look of surprise, she knew it was too late.

* * *

On Friday after work, Caitlin lay by the side of the pool, enjoying the cool breeze that rustled the trees. She watched, entranced, as the multi-coloured birds danced from tree to tree, calling to each other. She was beginning to see what Brianna loved about living here, although she found the heat difficult to cope with. Even though it was early evening it was still hot and Caitlin felt a trickle of perspiration trickle between her breasts. For a moment she thought of Ireland, the green fields and rolling hills—and the rain. She'd never thought she'd miss that, but after a week of endless sunshine she realised she did.

Brianna had gone to collect the children at a play date, refusing Caitlin's offer to accompany her, saying that she wanted to catch up with one of the mothers. As Niall's plane wasn't due for a couple of hours, Caitlin had the place to herself.

Although she loved her sister and her family dearly, Caitlin revelled in the peace and quiet. The first since she had arrived.

She glanced across at the pool. The water looked so cool and inviting. Making up her mind, she slipped off her shorts and T-shirt, followed quickly by her underwear—there was no one about to see her after all—and jumped into the pool, gasping with delight as she felt the cool water on her skin. She swam a few lengths underwater and then stopped to catch her breath. Good grief, she was out of shape. She must remember to ask Brianna if there was a gym she could join.

As a shadow fell across the pool she looked up to find Andrew standing by the edge of the pool, looking down at her. He had the sun at his back so she was unable to read his expression, but realising she was naked she wrapped her arms around her body. Did no one knock in this country?

He must have read her mind as he said, 'The front door was open so I thought I'd find you round the back.' He grinned down at her. 'I had no idea I'd find you skinny dipping,' he drawled, his Australian accent stronger than ever. 'Do you mind if I join you?' He was wearing a T-shirt and the same Bermuda shorts he had worn the previous weekend. Caitlin felt warmth deep in her belly.

'No,' she said sharply. 'I mean, yes, I do mind!'

'Too bad,' he said, grinning broadly, and with one sweep he had removed his T-shirt, revealing his muscular chest. Caitlin struggled to keep her eyes off his abdomen. She had seen six packs before, but never outside a magazine. He wasn't over-muscular, just perfect. Before she had a chance to protest further, he had dived in. At least he'd kept his Bermudas on, Caitlin thought. The image of them in the water together both naked was too much.

'Excuse me,' she said as he surfaced, water steaming from his black hair. 'I thought I said I didn't want you to come in. Now, either you get out or I will.'

'You're welcome to get out any time,' he said, his eyes creasing at the corners. 'Don't let me stop you.'

'You know I can't,' she protested.

'I won't look,' he said, and Caitlin heard the laughter in his voice.

'I don't care what you say,' Caitlin said fiercely. 'I'm not getting out until I'm sure you're nowhere in sight.'

'Okay,' he said lazily. 'Then you'll just have to stay there until I've finished my swim.' He turned on his stomach and started swimming. Caitlin didn't know what to do. It was ridiculous, being caught here in the pool, completely naked, while he swam up and down without a care in the world. What if Brianna returned with the children and found her in this intolerable situation? It just didn't bear thinking about. Then, to her alarm, she heard the sound of a car pulling up in front of the house.

'Andrew,' she snarled. 'Brianna and the children are back. Will you please get out and pass me a towel?'

Andrew looked at her and for a second Caitlin thought he was going to refuse, in which case there would be nothing for it except for her to take her chances and run for her clothes. But he seemed to take pity on her. He heaved himself out of the pool in one swift movement. As he did so, Caitlin was acutely conscious of his muscles bunching and the crease low on his back. He strode across to her lounger, grabbed a towel and passed it to her, turning his back as she got out of the pool. Wrapping herself in the towel, she had just enough time to snatch her clothes and make it to the downstairs cloak-room before she heard the sound of the children's laughter as they came into the kitchen. As she closed the door she heard a splash as Andrew dived back in to the water. She would make him pay for this, she promised herself.

By the time she had made herself presentable, Brianna was in the kitchen, fixing supper. Andrew was nowhere in sight.

'Niall's plane arrived early,' Brianna told her. 'Andrew offered to go and collect him. He's so sweet.' Sweet was the last thing Caitlin would have called him, but she resisted the impulse to tell her sister exactly what she thought of the man they were so friendly with. 'Don't you think he's lovely?' Brianna went on, oblivious to Caitlin's scowl.

Caitlin started chopping some chicken for the Caesar salad. 'Mmm,' she said. 'He's a little…' She struggled to find the right word. 'Too male for my liking.' It wasn't exactly what she meant, but it was the nearest she could think of without actually swearing.

'Too male?' Brianna said, looking amused. 'Yes, I can see why you would say that, but he's a real softy inside.'

Caitlin looked at her sister, perplexed. 'Are all Australian men like him?' she asked.

'You'll find Australian men are a breed unto themselves, but under that macho image, as you call it, they are real gents. And Andrew is no exception.' Brianna looked at her sister, narrowing her eyes. 'Hey, don't tell me you're falling for him.'

'Of course I'm not falling for him.' Caitlin laughed but even to her own ears the sound was hollow.

'Good, because, as I told you, he is strictly out of bounds. And, Caitlin, although I would love to see you and Andrew together, I also know that he could break your heart. For all your medical competency, I don't think you've ever had experience of a man like him.' She arched her eyebrow at her sister. 'He's as unlike David as it is possible for him to be.'

Before Caitlin had a chance to reply, the children came running in wet from the pool. Siobhan wrapped her wet arms around Caitlin's legs. 'I'm so glad you're here, Aunty Cat. Come and swim with me.'

Happily Caitlin was saved from having to disappoint her niece—having just washed her hair, she wasn't ready for another dip—by the sounds of Andrew and Niall returning from the airport. Siobhan abandoned her aunt and flung herself into her father's arms, competing with Ciaran for attention. Niall picked up both his children and leaned across and kissed his wife. Once again, Caitlin could almost feel the love that passed between them. Andrew stood to the side, watching closely. Caitlin thought she saw something move behind his eyes. What was it—sadness, envy?

Brianna insisted Andrew stay for supper and afterwards as the children watched TV, the adults moved out to the veranda with their coffee. Although the sun had long set, the air was still humid. Caitlin fanned herself with a newspaper she found on the table. 'When does it get cooler?' she asked.

'I'm afraid it only gets hotter from now until after Christmas,' Niall said, 'but you'll adapt to the heat eventually. Everyone does.'

'What if we all go to the Green Mountains tomorrow and stay the night? I was telling Caitlin about O'Reilly's the other day,' Andrew suggested. 'It's much cooler up there, and Caitlin will get a chance to see a rainforest. It's only just over an hour away from here.' He sat back, looking pleased with his suggestion. Niall and Brianna exchanged glances.

'Why don't just the two of you go?' Brianna suggested. Caitlin was horrified at the proposition. The last thing she wanted was to find herself alone with Andrew.

'Oh, I don't want to leave you on your own the first weekend,' Caitlin protested.

'Uh, Caitlin,' Andrew said quietly. 'I think Niall and Brianna might want a night on their own. After all, Niall has been away several days.'

Caitlin was mortified. She slid a look at her sister, who was blushing. 'I'm sorry, Bri,' she said. 'I wasn't thinking.' She thought for a moment. 'What if we take the children with us?

If Andrew's okay with that? It would give you and Niall a night on your own. A chance to sleep late. It will also give me some time with the children.' It was a good idea, she thought. Brianna and Niall probably hadn't many opportunities to spend time alone together. And taking the children along meant she wouldn't be alone with Andrew, as well as giving her the opportunity to get to know them again. Besides, she was keen to see more of this fascinating country. She glanced at Andrew, but in the dim light she was unable to read his expression.

'Sure, we can take the kids. You know I'm happy to help. If I remember, there's a lot for children to do up there.'

Brianna smiled broadly, the tiredness that seemed to haunt her disappearing from her face. 'Are you sure?' she said. 'That would be wonderful. I love my children, but they can be exhausting. Are you sure you two know what you're letting yourselves in for?'

'I think Caitlin and I can cope with most things,' Andrew drawled. He stood to leave. 'Well, that's settled. If they have room for us, the four of us will go up tomorrow. We can stay the night and come back on Sunday. Much as I love your children, I think one night would be enough.' He pulled out his mobile and searched for a number. After a few moments he was put through, and spoke for a few minutes. 'Yep. They can take us,' he said. 'I'll collect everyone about ten. Is that okay?'

'I think you've forgotten something,' Niall said, grinning. He looked pleased at the thought of having his wife to himself even for a short time. 'There is no way you're going to fit four people into your soft-top.'

'I hadn't thought that far,' Andrew admitted.

'You'll take our car, naturally,' Brianna said. 'You'll need it to cart the kids and all their gear.'

As they waved Andrew away, Caitlin found that the thought of a night away in Andrew's company was having a very disturbing effect on her pulse.

True to his word, Andrew arrived at ten to pick up Caitlin and the two children. It had taken the whole of the morning to organise the children. They had rushed around the house in a frenzy of excitement, refusing to stop long enough to have their faces washed or their hair brushed. However, after finally being threatened with having the whole trip called off, they had allowed themselves to be made ready. Caitlin felt exhausted already. If this was what having children meant, she was more sure than ever that it wasn't for her. Much better to have nieces and nephews who she could enjoy in small doses.

Seeing to the children had left Caitlin little time to get herself ready. In the end she had flung some walking boots, a bikini and a change of clothes into an overnight bag, adding a sweater at the last minute when Brianna had insisted.

'It gets cool in the mountains at night. You'll be surprised.' And so she would be. She was already beginning to feel like a washed-out rag in the heat. She couldn't imagine any part of Australia being cool enough for her to need extra clothing.

Andrew, on the other hand, looked fresh and cool in light-coloured trousers and a short-sleeved white shirt. He was wearing sunglasses, but that didn't stop Caitlin from noting his look of horror when he saw how much Brianna had packed for the night.

'You and Niall aren't planning to abscond while we are away?' he said, and Caitlin could tell he was only half joking. 'Because let me tell you, guys, as much as I am fond of your children there is no way I could survive more than one night with them.'

'Hey,' said Brianna, pretending to be affronted. 'Would I ever want to be without my children?' She smiled, but not before Caitlin saw a shadow flit across her eyes. Despite the brave way she was confronting her illness, she must inevitably think that there was always the possibility she wouldn't be around to see her children grow up.

But she brightened up again as she and Niall, their arms around each other, watched their children pile into the car. Several trips back to the house for forgotten toys and must-have books later and they were heading out of Brisbane.

'Only an hour late,' Andrew said, glancing at his watch. 'Not bad.'

'Do you have nieces and nephews?' Caitlin asked. 'Coming from a large family, I have several.'

'I'm an only child,' Andrew replied. For a

moment, Caitlin thought he was going to say something else but he seemed to change his mind.

'I can't imagine what that is like. With there being five of us, there was always so much activity in the house. It meant having to share, and often do without, as my parents weren't very well off, but the bonus was we always had someone to play with. And now that we're all older, we're still close.'

'Tell me about Ireland,' Andrew said. 'I've never been there.'

As they drove, Caitlin told Andrew about her life on the farm, how, when farming had become too difficult, her parents had changed direction and started breeding horses, which had turned out to be surprisingly successful. She told him about her three brothers and their families. Then, before she knew it, they were climbing the steep road into the mountains.

'I'm sorry,' she said. 'I must have bored you silly, going on like that.'

Andrew grinned at her.

The children, who had been listening to stories on a tape, perked up as they drove through the trees and emerged at the top of a mountain. Caitlin wound down the window and let the smell of eucalyptus waft in through the window. Flocks of vividly coloured parrots perched on every tree. Caitlin had never seen anything quite like it. As they got out of the air-conditioned car, Caitlin noticed that the air was noticeably cooler, and she sighed with pleasure. Within minutes they were surrounded by a gaggle of bush turkeys with their incongruous red and yellow necks. Gingerly Caitlin edged away from their pecking beaks as they scavenged for scraps.

Andrew laughed at her obvious discomfort as the children scampered away, shrieking with excitement.

'Hey, kids, come back,' Caitlin shouted. What if they fell down the steep slope in front of them? What if they hurt themselves? What if they got lost? She was beginning to regret that she had agreed to this trip. What did she know about looking after children? Although she loved her five nieces and nephews at home, their parents were always around to help. In fact, Caitlin realised with a pang of guilt, she had never taken time to do something with them. Tried to get to know them. She had always been too busy. It had taken something as serious as her sister's illness for her to spend time with these two. But feeling guilty didn't stop Caitlin feeling totally out of her depth.

As she started to run after them, Andrew caught her arm. 'Relax,' he said. 'Let them blow some steam off after the journey. They'll be fine.'

Feeling ridiculously out of her depth, she followed the children over to where the ground fell away. Beneath them she could see the canopy of the rainforest and in the distance the suspended walkway that Andrew had told her about. The one that would take them right across the top of the rainforest. Andrew unloaded their bags and joined her. The children, having lost interest in the rainforest, had discovered an adventure playground and had rushed off to join the children already there.

'It's beautiful,' Caitlin breathed, taking in the view of the mountains in the distance. 'We could be on our own small island here. It's like nothing I have ever seen before.'

'Come on,' Andrew said, appearing delighted with her reaction. 'Let's check in and have some lunch.'

After checking in, they were shown to their rooms. Caitlin was to share the larger of the two with the children, while Andrew had a smaller double to himself. Both had decks overlooking the rainforest and fireplaces. Andrew's even had a hot tub on his deck. Caitlin was glad she'd remembered to pack her bikini.

'We'll round up the children and then go for a walk,' Andrew suggested. But the children were against that plan. They had made friends who were going to the children's club and begged to be allowed to go too.

Caitlin hesitated. Would it be safe to leave them? After all, she was here to watch them and spend time with them. 'I think you should come with Uncle Andrew and me,' she said.

'Do we have to?' Siobhan moaned.

'I want to stay here,' Ciaran added, his mouth set in a mutinous line.

Once again Andrew intervened. He pulled

Caitlin out of earshot. 'Let them stay. The playground is supervised. The children need some time to have fun. I know they're both too small to understand what's going on with Brianna, but they are bound to have picked up that something isn't quite right. Let them just have fun for a little while.'

'Okay,' Caitlin conceded. But she was thinking that it was unfair that this man, for all his machismo, seemed to have a better understanding of her niece and nephew's needs than she did. Maybe it was something to do with being a paediatrician. He would have to be good with children to do his job well. In her speciality it was different. Once the babies were safely delivered, she had little to do with them. Hers was an adult speciality. Maybe she should trust his judgement. It was obvious to her he was far more relaxed around them than she was.

So after a very quick lunch, when the children hardly stayed still long enough to eat more than a couple of mouthfuls, she changed out of her shorts and into long trousers and hiking boots. Andrew had warned her about the insects on the forest floor. As soon as they had waved goodbye to Siobhan and Ciaran they set off down a steep track. As they descended the forest became denser, obscuring the sun. 'That's why they call it a canopy,' Andrew informed Caitlin. They followed the stream, the sound of water becoming louder with every step. Soon they came into a clearing where a waterfall tumbled down moss-covered rocks into the stream. A sudden movement startled Caitlin and she grabbed Andrew's arm. She found herself staring into the amber eyes of a brightly coloured toad, or frog—she didn't know the difference.

'You can let go now, if you like,' Andrew suggested. 'I don't think we're in any danger.'

Caitlin was mortified to find she was still clutching his arm. She could feel the heat of his skin under her fingers and the hard muscle of his forearm. She dropped her hand to her side.

'I thought it was a snake or some other beastie,' she apologised. 'I don't do those.'

'They will be more scared of you then you of them, I promise,' Andrew said.

'It seems that whenever I'm around you, I act

like some sort of pathetic female out of the nineteenth century.' She laughed to cover her embarrassment.

'I don't think you're pathetic at all,' Andrew said. 'In fact, I can imagine you more of a suffragette. Determined and tough, and not frightened of much, I would say.' Something in the tone of his voice sent a shiver of electricity down Caitlin's spine. The air crackled between them and she felt herself sway towards him. But then, just as quickly, the atmosphere changed. Andrew dropped his hand and moved away from her. Caitlin knew he was feeling whatever it was that lay between them. He was as attracted to her as she was to him. But she realised it was too complicated for them to start a relationship. They worked together, he was a family friend, godfather to her nephew, and then there was that strange comment from Brianna. The one about her not being Andrew's type. All in all, whatever it was that lay between them was best left unexplored.

They walked for a couple of hours before turning round and strolling back the way they'd come. They chatted easily about work, and Andrew told her about his holiday cottage on the Sunshine Coast, just over an hour's drive from Brisbane. 'I try to go up at least twice a month,' he said. 'About the same number of times I do a clinic up there. You are welcome to use it whenever you like,' he offered.

'Thank you,' Caitlin replied. 'I might just take you up on the offer, if Brianna and the family would come too. You said I'll be doing a clinic or two up there as well?'

'We'll probably do it at the same time. In many ways it's sensible to have a paediatrician and obstetrician there together. It can save time and unnecessary trips for patients. In fact, I'm scheduled to do one next Friday. I can find out whether they've rostered an obstetrician in and ask if you can take their place. You can stay at the cottage as my guest. I could show you around on Saturday.'

Caitlin wasn't at all sure whether a night in Andrew's company on her own was a good idea. But she told herself not to be absurd. He was behaving just as she would expect a colleague who knew the family would. There was no reason to read anything more into it.

'We'll see,' she said. 'It depends on Brianna and Niall and their plans for the weekend. I don't want them to feel abandoned. But whatever, I'd love to do the clinic if that's a possibility.'

After dinner Caitlin put the children to bed. Happily they were exhausted after their afternoon's excitement and soon drifted off. Andrew had suggested Caitlin might like to use the hot tub on his deck. His room was right next door to hers so they would hear the children if they woke up.

Caitlin slipped on her bikini and popped on the bathrobe that had been thoughtfully provided. The sun was turning the mountains purple and she stood on her balcony and watched as the sun slipped below the horizon. Despite all her worries about her sister she felt more at peace than she had been since she had heard the news. David had been dismayed when she had insisted on coming out here for six months, and when he'd refused to support her decision, Caitlin had realised that he wasn't the man she thought he was. Their break-up had brought surprising relief and Caitlin knew, if she was honest with herself, that she had been using her work to avoid him for a while. The break-up had been amicable, but Caitlin had wondered if she would ever meet that special someone who would make her heart race. Much in the same way Andrew did. But that was ridiculous, she told herself. She hardly knew the man. He wasn't her type, he lived thousands of miles away from her home, and—this was the biggie—she, according to her sister, had no chance with him.

The air was much cooler now that the sun had set, and Caitlin shivered. She knew that if Andrew had tried to kiss her back there in the forest she would have kissed him back. She had wanted him to kiss her. She had wanted to feel his lips on hers, his chest against hers. She was in lust. There was no denying the horrible truth. For the first time ever she had allowed a man to get under her skin and she didn't know how she felt about that. Not good, came the immediate reply from that part of her brain that was still capable of rational thought. Not good at all.

She knocked on Andrew's door. He had changed into jeans and a long-sleeved T-shirt. He also seemed oblivious to the fact he had a smear of soot on his forehead. He looked as sexy as hell, Caitlin thought.

'I'm putting on a fire,' he said. 'It's pretty cool now the sun has set.'

'I can see that. You men just like making fires.' Caitlin laughed. 'Hang on just a moment.' She licked her finger and, standing on tiptoe, reached up to wipe away the soot. As she leant towards him her bathrobe fell open. His hands reached down and encircled her waist, but only for a second. She saw surprise in his eyes, followed closely by something else—could it be desire?

'I'll just have a quick soak while you sort the fire out.' She was dismayed to find she was almost breathless. She walked over to the tub and shed her bathrobe, placing her glasses by the side. But just before she stepped into the bubbling water, she noticed something fat and wriggly attached to her ankle. She peered at it in disgust. It seemed to be a worm of some description. She smothered a shriek of disgust and tugged, planning to fling the disgusting thing as far as she could. But the creature, it seemed, had other ideas. Now it was attached to her it seemed it had no intention of letting go. She couldn't bear it any longer. Andrew must have caught the edge of her surprised squeak as he left the fire and came over to her.

'Everything all right?' he asked.

The last thing Caitlin wanted was for him to have to come to her rescue again, but the thought of spending the rest of the evening with an insect attached to her foot was equally un-bearable.

'There's a worm or something stuck on my foot! I can't get it off!'

'Here, let me see,' he said quietly. 'Sit down on the chair over there.'

Caitlin hopped over to the chair.

Andrew took her foot in his lap. With one swift yank he had removed the offending visitor from Caitlin's foot. Immediately blood began to ooze. He examined the insect with interest.

'It's a leech, but it's gone now,' he said. 'Remember I suggested that you tuck your trousers into your socks on our walk? This is the reason why.'

'Ugh,' Caitlin said forcefully. All of a sudden she became aware that her foot was still in his lap and she was wearing nothing but her tiny bikini. She felt Andrew's eyes flicker over her body. Slowly they took her in, from the tip of her toes, before coming to rest on her face. Every nerve in her body seemed to be tingling under his look. Abruptly he lifted her foot from his lap and stood.

'We can stick a plaster on it. Reception's bound to have one. I'll just nip across and get one,' he said.

'It's okay,' Caitlin said, scrambling to her feet. 'It'll stop bleeding soon enough.' But it looked as if Andrew couldn't wait to get away from her. Grief, did he think this was some half-baked attempt to seduce him? How mortifying.

'It won't stop bleeding for a while,' he said. 'These guys have anticoagulant in their bites. It's hardly life-threatening, but we don't want you to bleed all over the place, do we?' And with that he left the room.

Giving up on the hot tub, Caitlin retreated to her room, showered quickly and slipped on a pair of jeans and a thin cashmere sweater. While she showered she felt herself flush at the memory of her foot in his hand and his eyes on her body. Whatever this thing between them was, she knew he felt it too. She had thought he was going to kiss her and then he had pulled away. Clearly he was reluctant to start anything between them. Was it because they worked together? In that case, she could understand. But could she? They were both adults. Surely, at the grand age of twenty-nine, she could be expected to behave like one. Maybe it was more to do with him being friends with Brianna and Niall? That she could understand. It would be intensely awkward if anything did happen and then one of them broke it off. And, besides, Caitlin told herself firmly, she didn't want a relationship with a man who lived on the other side of the world from her. There was no future in it. And then there was Brianna. She was here to be with her sister, not be distracted by some man, no matter how gorgeous. She would put any feelings she might have aside and behave towards him as she would towards any other colleague. Why, then, did a little voice tell her that it wasn't going to be that easy?

While Andrew waited for the receptionist to fetch him a plaster, he too was thinking about Caitlin. Why did Brianna's sister have to be so sexy and warm and funny? She was doing things to his libido that he couldn't remember happening before. Sure, he'd had lovers. Sure he'd been fond of them, but they all knew the score and were happy to be lovers until the relationship came to a natural end. Which it always did. And he had to admit usually because he lost interest. But Caitlin was different. He knew deep in his heart that if he allowed her to get under his skin—more under his skin than she already was—she would be a difficult woman not to fall in love with. And falling in love wasn't part of his plans. It wouldn't be fair to her, it wouldn't be fair to him. They could never be anything more than lovers. Deep in his soul he knew that that wouldn't be enough for her. And to complicate matters further, she was Brianna's sister. He couldn't do anything but play fair with her.

Accepting the plaster from the receptionist, he made his way back to his room. Whatever this attraction was between him and Caitlin, he had to put an end to it. He would tell her the truth. It would be her call. If she wanted to take things further, knowing there was no future in it, who was he to stop her? Satisfied that he was doing the right thing, he felt his spirits rise. He would tell her, then leave it up to her.

But when he got to his room, Caitlin was nowhere to be seen. He felt an inordinate sense of disappointment and realised that he'd been hoping that she'd be there waiting for him, happy to pick up where they'd left off. But it seemed that for whatever reason she had decided against it. But she would still need the plaster. Tentatively, so as not to wake the children, he tapped on her door. She opened it, looking wary.

'I have the plaster,' he said. 'I thought you'd still be in my room.'

'I didn't think it was a good idea,' she said, her green eyes glinting. 'I'm tired, I guess I didn't realise how tired till just now. It was an early start, so if you'll excuse me, I think I'll just go to bed.' She held out her hand and took the plaster. Andrew felt crazily disappointed. He knew then he'd been hoping against hope that Caitlin would listen to what he had to say, and that it wouldn't make a difference. But it seemed she had different ideas. Had he read the situation all wrong? He was still thinking of what to say when she quietly but firmly closed the door on him.

CHAPTER FIVE

THE next morning Caitlin was woken by two small faces staring down at her. As she focused, Siobhan and Ciaran giggled.

'We've been waiting ages for you to wake up,' Siobhan said. 'Mummy said we weren't to wake you up, but we've been up for ages.'

Caitlin scrambled for her watch and squinted at the face. Five-thirty. She groaned. It was still the middle of the night! However, realising that the children would never allow her to go back to sleep, she eased herself out of bed. The children had tried to dress themselves, but had made rather a poor attempt at it. Siobhan was wearing a pair of shorts and a dress *and* Ciaran had his T-shirt on the wrong way round.

'Okay, guys, let me just make myself some

coffee and then I'll sort you out. After that we'll
go for breakfast—okay?'

While Caitlin waited for the kettle to boil she
fixed the children's clothes. Then, still in her
dressing gown, she opened the curtains and let
herself out onto the deck, coffee in hand. Dawn
was just beginning to light the sky and a heavy
mist hung over the trees. The birds had woken
and she listened to the strange chirping and
whirling cries as she sipped her coffee. It was
like being in another world, on another planet
even, she thought.

When she'd finished her coffee, she realised
that it had gone unnaturally quiet in the room.
She looked around feverishly but the children
were nowhere to be seen. An open door suggested that they had got tired of waiting for her
and had decided to go exploring. Caitlin flung
on her jeans and T-shirt and not stopping long
enough to pull a comb through her hair went off
in pursuit. How could she have turned her back
on them, even for a moment? Visions of them
being lost in the rainforest or slipping down the
side of a mountain, or, even worse, falling over

the edge of the canopy walk made her blood run cold. God, couldn't her sister rely on her for even twenty-four hours? If having children meant having eyes in the back of your head and being on alert twenty-four seven then Caitlin knew she had been right not to go down that route. Clearly she'd be a hopeless parent. Nieces and nephews, preferably at a distance, suited her just fine.

But she had only got as far as the room next to hers when she saw that the door was open. Hearing the sound of giggles, she followed the sound into Andrew's room to find him sitting up in bed looking bemused, a child on either side.

'They got you too, huh?' Caitlin said. The sight of him, all bleary-eyed and looking so aghast, made Caitlin laugh out loud.

'The last time I was awake this early I was on call,' Andrew admitted. 'Hey, I don't suppose you could make some coffee while I get dressed?' He flung aside the sheet, and Caitlin turned away, but not before she caught a glimpse of his torso. Her heart thudding, she busied herself with the coffee while, behind her, she heard him pad towards the shower. 'Give me five minutes,' he said.

His coffee was cooling by the time he emerged from the shower, a towel slung low on his hips. Caitlin couldn't help but look at his muscular chest, golden in colour and perfectly smooth. She was aware of his arms and the muscles that made it seem as if he worked out. Probably all that kite surfing, she thought. For a second she let herself imagine her head against his chest and his strong arms around her. She shook her head to chase away the image. That way lay madness.

By the time they made their way to the dining room, breakfast was being served and Caitlin saw to the children before helping herself to a plate of fruit, some of which she hadn't seen before. Nevertheless it was all delicious. Andrew tucked into a plate of bacon and pancakes. Catching Caitlin's look of amazement at how much he seemed able to pack away, he raised an eyebrow. 'I need to keep my strength up,' he said between mouthfuls. 'I have a feeling I'm going to need it today.'

'What's the plan?' Caitlin asked, rescuing Ciaran's tumbler just in time to stop it tipping over.

'I thought we should take the children on the canopy walk,' he said. 'It's an easy one, so they'll manage fine. After that, lunch and home, I guess. I told Brianna we'd have them back around three.'

'Sounds good to me,' Caitlin said.

'Me too,' said Siobhan. She looked just like Brianna had as a little girl, Caitlin thought. All red curls and freckles. Thinking about her sister, she remembered why she was here. Please, God, she sent a silent prayer heavenwards. Don't let anything bad happen to this family.

'How's your foot, by the way?' Andrew asked, helping himself to another slice of toast. Then he peered at her. 'Are you all right? You looked so sad there.'

'My foot's fine,' she said. 'And so am I.' She glanced pointedly in the direction of the children. Andrew was quick to pick up the signal. He must have guessed she was thinking about Brianna. He leaned over and touched her hand. It was only the lightest of touches but it sent an electric shock up Caitlin's arm. Before she could help herself she jerked it away.

The children, having finished their breakfasts, were growing restive. 'Let's go. Now!' Ciaran demanded. Andrew and Caitlin shared a look of resignation before gathering up the children.

'Surely among the treetops there are no jellyfish or leeches,' she said. 'I think I've had my share of troublesome Australian wildlife for the time being.'

'Don't worry,' Andrew said, grinning at her. 'You'll be perfectly safe.'

The canopy walkway snaked across the top of the trees. They had to cross a series of suspension bridges and there were viewing platforms along the way. The children kept shrieking with delight every time they spotted a different bird. Every now and again there would be sounds like a whip cracking or a rifle shot that made them all, but especially Caitlin, jump. Amused, Andrew explained the sounds were made by birds and that Caitlin shouldn't worry as there were no hunters in the forest waiting to take a potshot at her.

Although it was still early, the sun was already warming Caitlin's skin. At least up here the sun wasn't so unbearable. In fact, the heat was just perfect. As the children ran ahead Andrew said, 'You were thinking of Brianna back there—at breakfast—weren't you?'

Caitlin nodded. 'You could tell?' she asked, smiling wryly.

'You show everything in your face,' he said. 'Every emotion is written there for the world to see.'

Caitlin cringed inwardly. She certainly hoped not every emotion was visible—the last thing she wanted was for him to see how much he was affecting her.

'I guess I'm not as good at hiding my emotions as I thought I was,' she replied. 'Just as well I always tell my patients the truth. Otherwise they'd know immediately when I was lying and lose faith in me. But sometimes I wish I could switch off, not be so involved. I don't think I could be a paediatrician for that reason,' she said. 'Perhaps that's why my career is following the path of academia,' she added thoughtfully.

'I find I have to keep my distance. I worry I'd let personal feelings cloud my judgement otherwise,' Andrew answered.

Caitlin felt herself bristling. 'I don't think I have ever let my feelings cloud my judgement,' she said, more sharply than she'd intended.

'Hey,' Andrew said. 'I wasn't implying that you did. We all have to cope in different ways. I think you're an excellent doctor. Certainly if I had a wife I'd want her looked after by you.'

'And have you? Ever had a wife, I mean?' Maybe that was what Brianna had meant. Of course he was probably involved. After all, it was unlikely that someone as gorgeous as him wouldn't have someone. Maybe he was divorced and that's what Brianna had meant about her not being his type? But what was she thinking, letting her imagination run away with her? She could just ask him.

'A wife?' He shook his head. 'Good God, woman, I'm too young for one of those.'

'How old are you, then?' she asked.

'I'll be thirty on Christmas Day.'

'Most people would say that's not too young to settle down.'

He looked at her sharply. 'What about you? You're twenty-eight or twenty-nine? You don't look it,' he added hastily, 'but you must be at least that to be where you are professionally.'

'I'm almost thirty,' Caitlin said. 'And, no, I've never met someone I wanted to marry. I don't expect to either.'

'What, never? Don't you want kids?' He sounded astonished, Caitlin realised. 'I want several!' he continued, laughing, but she noticed a flicker in his eyes. Probably thinks all women should be barefoot and pregnant in the kitchen, Caitlin thought to herself. But she didn't have to justify her decision—not to him or anybody else for that matter.

She looked across to where Siobhan and Ciaran were playing. 'I have five nieces and nephews. And I have my work. That's enough for me.' By this time Ciaran had moved to the side and was beginning to climb the barrier for a better view. For a moment she thought Andrew was going to say something else, but instead he simply nodded and turned his attention back to the children. He scooped Ciaran up and swung him onto his shoulders. 'Come on, little fella, let's go have some fun.'

It was past three by the time they pulled up outside the house. Brianna and Niall came rushing out to meet them and the children flung themselves into their parents' arms as if they'd been away for weeks instead of a single night. 'Honestly, sis,' Caitlin said. 'We didn't beat them or starve them. Although,' she muttered under her breath, 'I was tempted this morning when they woke me at half-five.'

'Siobhan, Ciaran. What did I tell you about not disturbing Aunty Caitlin too early?' Brianna scolded mildly. 'Sorry, Cat, children have no respect for the adult's need to sleep.'

Caitlin laughed. 'It was no problem. I enjoyed our trip very much.'

'Thanks so much to both of you,' Brianna said. She looked so much better for her night with

Niall, Caitlin thought. Brianna's cheeks were pink and her eyes sparkling. She knew how much she loved her children, but guessed the strain of keeping up appearances in front of them took its toll. She'd have to try and give Brianna more breaks.

'Are you coming in, Andrew?' Niall asked.

'No, thanks,' Andrew replied. 'I thought I might get some kite boarding in while there's a bit of a breeze. I was thinking Caitlin might fancy coming too and give windsurfing a go,' he said. 'In fact, we could all go.'

'I think I'll pass,' Brianna said. 'If you don't mind. But you go on. Niall could go with you too, if he likes.'

'I spend enough time away from my kids as it is,' Niall said firmly. 'And although it was a pleasure to be alone with you, my darling wife, I'd really like to spend this afternoon with my family. Or had you forgotten I'm away again tomorrow?'

'No, I hadn't,' Brianna said softly. 'Do you have to?' Then she shook her head. 'Oh, don't mind me,' she said. 'Of course you have to. I'm just being silly.'

Caitlin and Niall exchanged concerned glances. Brianna had been so resolutely cheerful up to this point. The touch of anxiety in her voice was unsettling. Andrew must have noticed it too. He walked over to her and felt her forehead and then her pulse. 'Are you feeling okay?' he asked.

'I've just got a bit of a headache. Nothing a bit of a lie-down won't sort out. Niall can look after the children while I do that, so go on, Cat, take Andrew up on his offer.'

But Caitlin felt strangely reluctant to leave Brianna.

'I'm sure Andrew has had enough of my company for the time being,' she said lightly. 'And, besides, I'm not sure if I'm ready to risk being stung again. Besides,' she went on, 'I was almost eaten alive by this enormous leech after walking in the rainforest. Perhaps I should stay indoors for a while.'

'Wuss,' said Andrew challengely. 'Well, they do say women from the northern hemisphere are more timid. But I know Brianna has a wetsuit you can borrow. That'll keep you warm and safe.'

'You can say what you like,' Caitlin said, unmoved. 'But I quite fancy lying by the pool with a good book for a couple of hours. Maybe another time?'

'Fine by me,' Andrew said. 'I'll see you tomorrow, then?' And he kissed Brianna and the children before leaping into his car and heading off.

Brianna went to lie down while Niall took the children to the park. Caitlin took her book out to the pool and read before having a dip. After an hour's nap Brianna appeared, carrying two tall glasses of cold orange juice. Caitlin sipped hers greedily, then pressed the ice-cold glass to her forehead.

'How are you feeling?' Caitlin asked her sister.

'Much better, thanks. It was only a headache.' She sat next to Caitlin and stretched out. 'Tell me about O'Reilly's,' she said. 'Did you love it?'

'Mmm,' Caitlin said. 'I thought it was wonderful. Maybe you and Niall could come the next time?'

'We'll see,' Brianna said. 'Anyway, although I promised not to pester you, did you get a chance to think about what I said? About getting yourself checked? I need to know you're all right.'

'Once the big sister, always the big sister.' Caitlin smiled. 'I did think about it, Bri, and I'll go for a mammogram—soon, I promise. Just to put your mind at ease if nothing else. But as for the genetic screening, I'm not sure there is any point. If I do have the gene, what then? I don't think I want to live my life knowing that the sword of Damocles was about to fall.'

Brianna took a deep breath. 'I've been thinking too,' she said. 'I spoke to Andrew about it. He knows someone who will carry out the test on me. I need to know if I carry the gene. I need to know because of Siobhan. Do you understand?'

Caitlin hugged her sister. 'You know I'll support you, whatever you decide,' she said. Then a thought struck her. 'But what if you do turn out to have the gene? What then?'

'I'll consider a mastectomy. Above all else I want to be alive for my children, whatever the cost.'

'It's a big decision,' Caitlin said slowly. 'Not one

I think I could make. But if you are going to be tested, then I suppose I should think about it too. If you come back positive, there's a good chance I'll also carry the gene. Whew! I hadn't really thought through all the ramifications before.'

'That's why I wanted to speak to you first. Because, whatever I do, it will affect you,' Brianna replied.

'Well, let's hope for all our sakes, not least Siobhan's, that it will all turn out fine.' She felt her voice shake and fought to keep her emotions under control. Then the two sisters were in each other's arms, crying as if their hearts would break.

Later, having cried themselves out, they broke apart, blew their noses and smiled at each other.

'I needed that,' Brianna said. 'I have been holding it together for Niall and the children, but I feel so much better for letting it all out.'

'Me too,' Caitlin said. 'I know you're scared, Bri. I would be too in your shoes, even though I know you're going to be fine. I hate to think of you going through all this. I feel so helpless. But we have to stay positive. Agreed?'

'Agreed. Enough emotional stuff for the time

being. Tell me, how did you get on with Andrew while you were away?'

'Fine. He's very…nice,' Caitlin said evasively, but as Andrew had pointed out she found it difficult to hide her feelings, especially from her sister.

'I was right,' Brianna, said. 'You fancy him!'

'He's good looking, I admit,' Caitlin said reluctantly, then catching her sister's eye, laughed. 'Okay, he's the sexiest man with the hottest body I have seen in a long time, but that doesn't mean I fancy him.'

Brianna sighed. 'I'm not sure I believe you, sis, but as I warned you before, don't get your hopes up in that direction.'

'I'm not!' Caitlin protested, crossing her fingers behind her back. 'I've told you many times before, I don't think I'm the kind of woman who is destined for a long-term relationship. I'm not sure I want kids so what's the point? Besides, if I want to get the chair of obstetrics then I need to concentrate on my career.'

'Are you sure that's still what you want? Didn't coming out here kind of spoil that for you? Besides, Cat, there's more to life than just work.'

'I know that! I have my family, my friends as well. I'm not a recluse, you know. As for the job, they very graciously agreed to this six-month sabbatical. The Queensland Royal is a pretty prestigious hospital and the Dublin Women and Children's likes their consultants to have international connections. Anyway,' she said, returning to the subject she had been thinking about, 'why shouldn't I get my hopes up? Am I so ugly that you think a hunk like him wouldn't be interested?'

Brianna laughed. 'You know as well as I do that you are beautiful—it runs in the family after all.'

'What, then? Has he been married? In a relationship? There's no sign of a woman on the scene.'

'There have been plenty on the scene, as you say, but not at the moment. Look, I don't know how much he told you about himself.'

'Not a lot,' Caitlin admitted. 'We mainly spoke about you guys—and work.'

'You know his parents are from India originally, although Andrew and his sister were born here.'

'I didn't know he had a sister,' Caitlin said surprised. 'He never mentioned her. Is she here too?'

'She was. Sadly she died after a difficult labour. She suffered an unexpected and catastrophic bleed after a stillbirth.' Brianna shuddered. 'I was on that day, in Theatre. It was awful. It broke everyone's heart. His in particular.' Brianna stopped and looked into the distance as if remembering.

'How tragic. Poor Andrew. Poor family. It's terrible that these things can happen even in this day and age.' She thought back to his words about not being too involved with patients, but it was bound to be there in his mind every time there was an obstetric emergency.

'He was very close to her. They were a close-knit family. Andrew was always the dearly loved only son, but when his sister died, his parents really started focussing on him. He became the centre of their universe. I'm surprised they haven't moved to Brisbane to be closer but I guess the family business makes it difficult for them to leave Sydney.' Caitlin waited for Brianna to continue. This was all very interesting and she felt a shock of sympathy for Andrew.

'Although we've known Andrew for ages he never talks about his sister's death. Or the rest of his family for that matter, although I know he visits his parents often. If his sister hadn't died at the Queensland Royal, I doubt I would even have known about her.' Brianna went on after a pause. 'I tried to raise the subject once, thinking he might need to talk about it, and nearly got my head in my hands.'

'Some men find it difficult to talk about the stuff that really hurts them,' Caitlin said.

'Sometimes I think it's the reason Andrew won't commit. Maybe he's frightened the same thing could happen again.'

'He's a doctor,' Caitlin argued. 'He must know the chances of lightning striking twice are slim, to say the least.'

'Ah, there you go, my dear sister. Assuming everyone thinks about things as rationally as you do. Where's your heart, woman?'

But Caitlin was beginning to wonder if she could think rationally any more. Not least when it came to Dr Andrew Bedi. And as for her heart? She ignored the warning voice in her head. No, her heart was still safe. Being in lust wasn't the same as being in love. Everyone knew that.

CHAPTER SIX

AFTER a fitful night tossing and turning, Caitlin gave up trying to sleep and instead got up early. It was so unlike her not to drop off as soon as her head hit the pillow. Perhaps it was concern for Brianna that had kept her from drifting off— because it certainly wasn't because Dr Andrew Bedi kept drifting into her dreams. She was attracted to him, she acknowledged that much, but that was as far as it went!

He was beginning to occupy far too much of her thoughts, Caitlin told herself crossly. Normally totally focussed on her work, she shouldn't be allowing that man to distract her— no matter how delicious he was to look at. As she let herself quietly out of the house, her thoughts once more turned to her duties. At least she could get a head start doing rounds of the

142 THE PLAYBOY DOCTOR'S SURPRISE PROPOSAL

labour suite and the antenatal ward before tracking down Patricia Levy, she reasoned. She had heard from one of the juniors that she was still in hospital, but due to be discharged later that day. Her baby was still in Special Care, making progress although still being ventilated.

Caitlin had been reluctant to leave Brianna, who still appeared under the weather, especially as Niall was off on another business trip, but her sister had insisted. 'It's only a touch of flu or something.' She had dismissed both her sister's and her husband's concern the night before. 'Away you go, both of you. You'll just drive me mad if you hang about hovering over me. I'm fine, trust me.'

Caitlin found her patient on the antenatal ward listlessly packing her few belongings. When she looked up and saw Caitlin she gave her a wan smile.

'How are you feeling?' Caitlin asked.

'Oh, I feel perfectly chucker,' she replied. 'I'm being discharged.'

'How's the little one?' Caitlin asked.

Immediately tears sprang to Patricia's eyes.

'They say she's holding her own.' She sniffed. 'But she's so small and defenceless. I can't bear to leave her here all by herself, but I need to go home and see my other kids. If Jack were here, he could stay with her while I'm away.'

Impulsively Caitlin hugged the distraught woman. 'Don't worry, we'll keep a very good eye on her for you,' she said. 'And if there's any change at all, we'll call you.'

'It's only for a few hours,' Patricia sniffed. 'They've given me a room to stay in when I get back. But what if something happens while I'm away?'

'Come on. Let's go and see how she is,' Caitlin said, trying not to look at her watch. She was due in Theatre, but she could see Patricia needed her right now. They took the lift up to the special care nursery. As before, it was a hive of activity with all the cots taken up. And, once again, there were anxious parents keeping vigil. Caitlin recognised one couple from a few days before. However, by the smiles on their faces, it appeared that their baby at least was making good progress. She followed Patricia over to her baby's cot and wasn't surprised to find Andrew's dark head bending over the infant. He looked up at their approach and instantly Caitlin could make out the concern in his eyes. She felt her heart sink. She couldn't bear it if anything happened to Patricia's baby.

Gently Andrew sat Patricia down. 'I'm afraid your baby took a turn for the worse a few minutes ago and we've had to put her back on the ventilator and sedate her again.'

Patricia looked up at him, stricken. 'Is she going to be all right?' she asked, her voice barely audible.

'We're doing everything we can,' he said.

Caitlin caught his eye again. She read pity in his deep brown eyes. It didn't bode well.

'I can't leave her now,' Patricia said. 'I'll need to phone my mum and let her know.'

'Give me the number,' Caitlin offered. 'That way you can stay here. I'll phone from the duty room.'

Patricia nodded gratefully. 'Tell Mum I'll phone her as soon as I have news,' she said, taking a deep breath. Her tears had dried up and there was new resolution in the squaring of her shoulders. 'I need to be strong—for my baby,' she said.

'I'll come back up and see you after my theatre list,' Caitlin said, blinking away the tears. Then she turned and headed towards the duty room. She had just finished relaying the news to Patricia's mother when Andrew came in.

'Are you all right?' he asked.

'Yes,' Caitlin said, struggling to keep her voice under control. 'How is Patricia's baby?'

'We've managed to stabilise her for the time being. She's a little fighter. We're doing everything we can. But all we can do at the moment is take each day at a time.'

'I know we shouldn't get emotionally involved, but Patricia has lost so much already. I don't think she could bear it if her baby doesn't make it.'

Andrew pulled Caitlin round to face him and looked directly into her eyes. 'I promise you that if there is any way on this earth that I can pull this baby through, I'll do it.' Caitlin returned his look. His nutmeg eyes burned with determination. She believed him.

'I know you will,' she said quietly. 'C'mon, let's get back in there.'

Later, after leaving an anxious Patricia by the side of her baby's cot, Caitlin made her way to the antenatal ward for rounds. Out of the ten women in the antenatal ward, most were doing well, although two needed to be taken to Theatre later that afternoon for elective sections. Neither woman was causing Caitlin much concern. The sections would be straight-forward, and she was able to reassure both that they would be holding their babies in their arms later that day.

Glancing at her watch, Caitlin saw that she had just enough time for a quick bite before Theatre and made her way to the hospital canteen. Selecting a salad, she realised that wherever in the world you were, canteens stayed the same. She had just finished the last mouthful when Andrew plonked himself down beside her.

'Hey,' he said. 'Busy morning?'

'You could say that,' Caitlin answered. 'I've a list starting in a few minutes.'

'Anything likely to cause problems?'

Caitlin shook her head and gave him a brief run-through of her cases. 'How's baby Levy?' she asked when she had finished.

'She's doing okay,' Andrew said. 'I'll go and see her again before I leave today. By the way,' he said as Caitlin picked up her tray, 'I'm scheduled to visit the clinic up on the Sunshine Coast on Friday. I thought you'd like to come along as the visiting obstetrician. Like I told you, we take turns to go up once a week to see any referrals the GPs have. We find that having a paediatrician and obstetrician there at the same time works well. The paediatricians see any of the kids that they want a specialist opinion on, and you guys see the pregnant ladies as well as the gynae stuff. If there's any problems with your pregnant ladies, one of us is about for a consult. The other specialties offer the same kind of service.'

'I'd love to go,' Caitlin said. 'I'll just need to make sure the labour ward is covered.'

'Done,' Andrew said. 'I saw Dr Menzies

earlier. He was scheduled to go with me, but he's more than happy to cover for you to go in his place.'

Caitlin raised an eyebrow. 'Don't you think it would have been better for me to have asked him? Really, Andrew, I'd much prefer to speak to my colleagues myself.'

'Hey,' Andrew said. 'I didn't mean to step on your toes. I just thought you'd like to come, and as I bumped into him I took the opportunity to check it out.'

Caitlin sighed, knowing that she was being unreasonable. Nevertheless, Andrew had to realise that she wanted to be seen as an equal part of the team. Not just some foreign doctor who swanned about the place, picking and choosing her cases.

'I won't do it again,' Andrew apologized, but Caitlin could tell from the glint in his eye that he wasn't perturbed in the slightest. It seemed as if Andrew Bedi was used to doing exactly as he pleased. 'Remember I told you that I have a house up there I use at weekends. I often stay over for the weekend when I'm up there. It isn't much, more like a cabin, but you'd be welcome to stay too.'

Caitlin's pulse began to race. The thought of spending a night alone with Andrew seemed tantalisingly tempting but dangerous.

'I don't know about staying,' she said slowly. 'I'd really like to spend the time with Brianna. It feels like I've hardly seen her.'

Andrew shrugged. 'No worries. It's up to you, of course. It was just a suggestion. But I can understand you might not want to be alone with me overnight.' This time there was a definite challenge in his dark eyes.

'Don't be ridiculous,' Caitlin retorted. 'That's got nothing to do with it.' She returned his stare. 'Anyway, I'm sure you'd prefer to have your house to yourself?'

She couldn't help but ask the question. Despite herself, she was desperately curious about Andrew's love life. She found it almost inconceivable that he wouldn't have a woman somewhere.

But it seemed that Andrew wasn't fooled by the forced casualness in her voice. He grinned, his teeth a flash of brilliant white against his dark skin.

'Are you asking?' he drawled. 'What is it you'd like to know about my love life, Dr O'Neill?'

'Of course I'm not the slightest bit interested,' Caitlin said, flustered. 'It was just a friendly question from one colleague to another. I'm assuming that we *can* be friends?'

He leaned forward. 'I don't know Caitlin. What do you think?' he said softly. Then he smiled and stood up. 'Let me know what you decide,' he said. 'If you decide to stay we can go in my car, if not, we'll need to take two.'

He left Caitlin sitting, her heart thudding in the most disconcerting manner. She felt she had been thrown a challenge, but what exactly it was she had no idea. Somehow the only thing she felt sure of was that no man had ever made her feel like this before. Perhaps the safest course was to keep as far away from Dr Andrew Bedi as possible. And the safe course was always what Caitlin preferred.

'Of course you should stay over,' Brianna insisted when she and Caitlin were on the veranda, enjoying the evening breeze. The children were in bed, dinner had been cleared away, and it was the first opportunity the sisters had had to catch up. 'Why shouldn't you?'

'Well, first off, the whole point of me being here is to spend time with you,' Caitlin said, smiling at her sister. 'We've missed so much time already. Secondly, it feels a bit strange, spending the night at Andrew's place. A bit too familiar, if you see what I mean.'

Brianna smiled wickedly. 'Putting the first reason aside for the moment, and remembering I don't want people behaving differently around me, it's the second that intrigues me. Don't you feel safe around Andrew? C'mon, 'fess up. What's going on?'

'Absolutely nothing is going on!' Caitlin protested. Then catching her sister grinning even more disbelievingly, she laughed. 'I can't help it, Bri. There's just something about him I find unsettling.'

'Nothing to do with the fact that he's gorgeous, has a body to die for, and is actually a really nice guy?'

'And, as you keep reminding me, unavailable.'

'Hey,' Brianna said, growing serious, 'I thought you weren't looking for a serious romance.'

'And I meant it. And somehow I don't think that's what Andrew wants either. Anyway, all of this is nonsense. I'm only here for a few months, and then it's back to Ireland. I really want the professorship and nothing and no one is going to stand in my way.'

'Hey, I'm not the one who's stressing. If there's nothing between you and Andrew, I don't see why you don't take him up on his offer.'

'I'll sleep on it,' Caitlin conceded. 'But you're right, we've spent enough time discussing Andrew Bedi.'

For the next few days, Caitlin was kept busy. She loved the ambiance of the hospital. The staff all went out of their way to make her feel welcome and she was impressed by the standard of care the hospital offered. She saw Andrew several times during the day. Often he'd be in Theatre with her for the more complex cases, and she found that they had an easy understanding when they worked together. Patricia's baby was improving every day. Caitlin was delighted when one day she found Patricia in the special care nursery, holding her baby in her lap. All the tubes had been removed and the blue tinge which had worried everyone so much had disappeared and had been replaced by a healthy pink.

Caitlin bent over the sleeping baby.

'She looks great,' she whispered.

'I can't believe how much she's improved in the last few days,' Patricia whispered back. 'I'll never be able to thank everyone. Especially Dr Bedi. He's been in to see her every day, at least twice, and as for the nurses—nothing has been too much trouble.'

'Have you decided on a name yet?'

'Do you have a middle name?' Patricia asked.

'Yes, I do. It's Colleen.'

'Colleen,' Patricia said, savouring the name. 'Then that's what I'm going to call her. Colleen—after you. It's a beautiful name and I think it suits her perfectly.'

Caitlin was touched by the gesture. 'I suppose

you couldn't call her Andrew.' She laughed. 'When do they think you'll get her home?'

'Colleen's to stay in for another week or two. At least until she puts on some weight. I've taken a room close by and the my boys are coming to stay with me. I've missed them so much. This way, I'll be able to see Colleen every day, as well as the other kids.'

By Thursday, Colleen had put on another two ounces, and Andrew told Caitlin he was confident enough about her progress to leave her in the safe hands of his colleagues while they were up north. On Friday morning they met as agreed at the hospital entrance. Caitlin was still undecided whether to stay the night at Andrew's place, but had packed a small bag, just in case.

'If you decide against staying,' Andrew said, 'I'll drive you back. But you should make the most of the opportunity while you can.' He grinned at her. 'Don't worry, you'll be perfectly safe.'

Caitlin chose to ignore him, throwing her bag into the small boot and climbing into the car beside Andrew. Although it was still early, the morning sun was already scorching. Before long, they had left the city behind. As they drove, Caitlin couldn't stop herself exclaiming in awe and admiration. With the ocean on one side and mountains on the other, the scenery left her breathless. Andrew had let down the hood and Caitlin revelled in the cool breeze as they drove.

'To think that back home it's pouring with rain,' she said. 'When I spoke to Mum this morning she said it hadn't stopped for the last few days.'

'Sometimes it gets so hot,' Andrew replied, 'that we'd do anything to have your weather for a day or two.' Then he looked at her and grinned. 'But only for a day or two.'

The clinic was in one of the health centres on the outskirts of town. By the time they arrived it was almost nine, and Andrew just had enough time to show Caitlin around before he disappeared to see his first patient.

The clinic nurse explained to Caitlin that they only scheduled the higher risk pregnancies and the first-time mothers for the specialist clinics.

All other patients saw the midwives and were admitted to the hospital in Brisbane only when they were near their delivery dates.

Her first couple of patients were straightforward. Excited new mums booking in with their first pregnancies. But neither of them were quite as excited as Caitlin's third patient. Amy Jordan was a pretty blonde with anxious blue eyes and a tentative smile. Her husband, Richard, looked slightly dazed.

Caitlin looked at her chart. Amy had had three rounds of IVF. The first two had been unsuccessful, but today after a third round, they were attending the clinic for a pregnancy test. The nurse had slipped the result to Caitlin along with the notes.

'Congratulations.' Caitlin smiled at her. 'Your test is positive.'

The couple in front of her just stared, looking as if they hardly dared believe what Caitlin was saying.

'Excuse me,' Amy said. 'But did you say the test was positive?'

'Yes, but remember it's very early days.'

But nothing was going to wipe the smile off

Amy's face. She turned to her husband. 'Did you hear what the doctor said? We're pregnant!' Her voice was low, hushed with barely contained excitement, as if she couldn't quite believe the news.

Then her husband jumped to his feet and, pulling his wife into his arms, swung her in a circle. The happy couple laughed, then as soon as Richard deposited Amy back on the floor she burst into tears. She sobbed for several minutes while her bewildered husband looked on helplessly.

'I don't know why I'm crying,' Amy sobbed. 'I'm so happy. I'm going to have a baby. After all this time!'

Caitlin smiled and passed Amy a box of tissues, giving her time to let the news sink in. As she watched the couple crying and laughing while they hugged, Caitlin wondered for the first time what it would feel like to want a child so much. She had never felt the need for children before, but what if, like the couple in front of her, that decision was taken out of her hands and she couldn't have children? How would that feel? She shook her head. What had prompted the thought? In all the years that she had been working as an obstetrician, she had never really considered a future where she might want kids. Why was the thought entering her mind now? She shook her head to clear it as Richard spoke.

'We've been trying for a baby for so long,' he told Caitlin. 'When it didn't happen at first we weren't too bothered. We just concentrated on having fun and setting up home together. But then after three years and it still hadn't happened we began to get worried, so we went to see our gynaecologist. He suggested IVF. This was to be our last go. If it failed we'd agreed to give up and get on with our lives.' His voice dropped. 'I'm going to be a dad. I can't believe it!' Caitlin could see he was struggling to stop his voice from breaking.

'As I said, it's very early days. We'll only truly know if the pregnancy is continuing at the first scan.' She made a note on the chart. 'I want you to come and see me in Brisbane in a few weeks for your scan. Will you do that?'

Eventually Amy and Richard left the consulting room. Even through the closed door, Caitlin could hear the cries of delight from the nursing staff mingling with those of the ecstatic couple. The next few weeks would be anxious ones she knew. Getting pregnant was only one stage in the difficult IVF journey. She desperately hoped that this couple at least would have the outcome they so badly wanted.

The rest of the day passed quickly. Most of the other patients were straightforward, except for the last woman, a patient who was thirty-six weeks pregnant and who the nurses wanted Caitlin to scan. They told Caitlin that they were a bit concerned that the baby wasn't the right size for its dates. Sure enough, when Caitlin scanned the baby she thought that the baby's heart looked abnormal. Unsure and concerned, she asked Andrew for a second opinion, thinking that it was lucky that he was the visiting paediatrician as she had remembered his special interest was in cardiac problems.

After examining the scan for a few minutes, he took Caitlin to one side. 'I think you're right,' he said. 'It looks as if there is a heart defect. But we need a better quality of scan before we can be sure. Although this machine is adequate for most stuff, we really need to scan her again with the one back at the hospital before I can check all the heart chambers properly.'

Not for the first time, Caitlin wondered about her chosen specialty. One minute you'd be giving patients the best news they had in years, the next you could be giving parents the worst possible news.

'I'll arrange for her to be seen at the Queensland Royal on Monday,' Caitlin said. 'We can scan her again then. But it doesn't look good, does it?'

Andrew shook his head. 'But there is no point in worrying them before we know exactly what we are dealing with here. And, if there is damage to the heart, at least we can make sure that we have the paediatric cardiac team available at delivery. Good call. If it hadn't been picked up and she had gone into labour up here, it could have been a different story.'

'I'll speak to them,' she said.

'We'll speak to them together,' Andrew said.

They returned to the patient, who was waiting anxiously, holding tightly to her husband's hand.

'Dr Bedi and I think it's possible that your baby has something wrong with its heart.' The patient, a young woman in her early twenties, went pale.

'Try not to worry too much at this stage,' Andrew said quickly. 'The abnormality could be something fairly minor. Like a hole in the heart, for instance.'

Seeing that this alarmed the patients even further, Caitlin added hastily, 'I know that sounds as if it's serious, but often it doesn't need treatment and the children go on to live normal productive lives.'

'And even if it turns out to be something that requires surgery, the fact that we know about it in advance means that we will have the full paediatric cardiac team standing by,' Andrew added. 'On the whole, it is very lucky that Dr O'Neill picked it up at this stage. It means that we can monitor your baby for the rest of the pregnancy and ensure that it gets the attention it needs at the right time.' Andrew hunkered down and held the woman's hand. 'I know it sounds scary right now, but you'll have to trust us. The first step is to arrange for you to be seen at the Queensland Royal and have a detailed scan on Monday. Dr O'Neill will arrange that for you, and we'll both see you then. Okay?'

The worried couple looked a little reassured but Caitlin knew that they would have an anxious wait over the weekend. She was very glad that Andrew had been there to check the scan with her. His experience and knowledge meant that he was able to reassure the patients much better than she would have been able to, had she been on her own. But it wasn't just his medical experience that she valued. Seeing the way he spoke to the patients, his obvious sympathy and understanding of their anxiety, at odds with the macho image he presented so much of the time, was revealing another side to a man that she was finding herself increasingly drawn to. More and more she was beginning to realise that she wasn't just attracted to Andrew because of his dark good looks and sex appeal, she was increasingly finding herself warming to

Andrew the man. And, as her heart tripped, she knew that spelled danger.

Later, once Caitlin and Andrew had finished writing up notes and making arrangements for the patients who needed to be seen back at the Queensland Royal, Andrew turned to Caitlin.

'Hungry?' he asked.

'A bit,' Caitlin replied, realising that these days, whenever she was around Andrew, food was the last thing on her mind. 'I don't know about you, but I didn't have time for anything at lunchtime except a quick coffee and an apple.'

'I managed a sandwich,' Andrew replied, 'but that's not enough for a busy man. I need something more substantial.'

'What do you have in mind?' Caitlin asked.

'There's a great seafood restaurant a few minutes' walk from my house. If you would agree to stay the night, we could stop at my place and grab a shower first. What do you think?'

'Dinner sounds good, but I don't think I could be seen anywhere without a shower,' Caitlin said. 'Or a change of clothes. So, okay, I'll stay.

Why not? I might not get another opportunity to explore the Sunshine Coast.' *Or another chance to see where Andrew lives, to learn more about the man who you can't seem to get out of your mind.* The voice in her head was back. Caitlin chose to ignore it.

Andrew's house was a wooden affair built on stilts. As Caitlin followed him up the steps to the main door she stopped and looked behind her. His house overlooked a stretch of beach that seemed to go on for miles. Apart from a solitary figure walking a dog, the white sands were deserted. Andrew's house was only one of about five as far as Caitlin could see.

'How on earth did you manage to find this place?' Caitlin said.

'My parents gave it to me,' Andrew said, turning to stand by Caitlin as she admired the view. 'It was their first home when they came to Australia over thirty years ago. Land out here was cheap back then, nobody wanted to live so far away from the city. And then before it became popular the government declared it a national park. No one else can build here.'

'I see why you come here as often as you can,' Caitlin said. 'I can't imagine a more beautiful place to live.'

Although he tried to hide it, Caitlin could tell that Andrew was pleased by her genuine admiration.

'I love it here,' he said. 'It's where I learnt to kite board and waterski and windsurf.' He pointed to a small cove to the right of the house. 'I keep my speedboat over there.' He turned to Caitlin. 'I don't suppose you fancy having a go?'

'What, right now?' He couldn't be serious surely? It wouldn't be long before it would be dark.

He grinned. 'You should try kite boarding in the moonlight,' he said. 'There's nothing to beat it. Just you, the sea and the moon.' He looked directly into her eyes. 'Don't you ever want to stop holding back and just let yourself go? Just have fun? Try new things? Don't you get just a little bit tired of being so, well, serious all the time?'

Caitlin took a sharp intake of breath. There was no mistaking the challenge in his deep brown eyes. Well, she would show him.

'Of course I know how to have fun,' she said defensively. 'I have fun all the time.' But as she frantically searched her mind for the last time she'd had fun, she realised that apart from the trip to the Green Mountains with Andrew she couldn't remember. She had been working so hard for so long, she had forgotten how to take time for frivolous activities. 'Right, then,' she said decisively. 'You're on.'

Andrew looked at his watch. 'I'll book dinner for eight—that will give us an hour or so on the water and time to change.'

'What?' Caitlin yelped. 'You mean go out now? I was thinking some time in the future.'

'No time like the present,' Andrew replied. 'Of course, if you're scared…?'

Caitlin had had about enough. Leeches and jellyfish aside, there was very little she was scared of. Well, very little she was going to admit to in front of this Neanderthal.

'I haven't brought a costume,' she managed, thinking that she had a genuine reason to turn down the challenge. But it seemed as if there was no way out.

'No worries. I have a wetsuit one of my...' He hesitated. 'My friends left behind.' His eyes raked her body. 'You look a similar size—a bit taller and more curvy perhaps, but I'm sure it will fit.'

Curvy? Who was he calling curvy? Okay, perhaps without the benefit of her daily swim she had put on a few pounds, but still—curvy? Caitlin was in no doubt what sort of friend had left a wetsuit behind. However, she reminded herself it was none of her business. She searched frantically for another excuse but, failing to find one, realised that there was nothing for it but to go through with whatever Andrew had in mind.

'Okay,' she said brightly, determined not to let her apprehension show. 'What do you have in mind?'

'You could try windsurfing. I have the board somewhere I used to use as a kid. It's perfect for a beginner. Or you could have a go waterskiing if you prefer. Actually, no, we really need a third person to act as a spotter, so we'll leave that for another day. Windsurfing it is, then. C'mon, let's get you suited up.'

Before she knew it, Caitlin was squeezing herself into a rubber suit. When at first it seemed as if there was no way it would go over her hips she was both mortified and then relieved. But then, with a final tug, the suit slipped past her hips and with a final sigh of resignation she slid her arms into the sleeves. Looking around for a mirror, she glanced around Andrew's bedroom. Simple pieces of wooden furniture lined two of the walls, but even with her limited knowledge of antiques Caitlin knew they were of exquisite quality. The beautiful oak floorboards were partially covered by a Persian carpet of rich jewel colours. Caitlin was slightly taken aback—she had somehow expected it to be masculine and Spartan. Instead it was warm and…she searched for a suitable description…comforting. Her eyes were drawn to the large double bed that dominated the room. No doubt he needed one of those, she thought waspishly. But no mirror. Perhaps it was just as well. Caitlin wasn't sure she wanted to see how she looked. Tentatively she peered into the small sitting room, looking for Andrew. Much like the bedroom, it was thoughtfully furnished, with two large, comfortable sofas arranged in an L facing the expanse of windows overlooking the sea. Plants and knick-knacks adorned the room. This wasn't a bachelor pad, Caitlin thought, it was a home. It seemed just as she was beginning to think she had him pegged, she found out something about him that made her revise her opinion. But not entirely. She wasn't surprised to see there was no television. As she suspected, Andrew didn't seem to be the sort of man who sat still long enough to watch a whole programme. He was just replacing the telephone receiver when he caught sight of her and grinned.

'Table booked,' he said. Then he crossed the room. 'Turn around while I do you up,' he said.

Caitlin felt goose-bumps all over her body as his fingers brushed the back of her neck.

'That's you,' he said, and whirled her around to face him. 'I don't think these are a good idea,' he added, removing her glasses. For a moment he looked into her eyes and her heart started thumping wildly. 'You have beautiful eyes,' he said. 'Why do you hide them behind these?'

Caitlin grabbed her glasses back, desperate for him not to see her reaction.

'I need those. I can't see very well without them.'

'What's there to see?' Andrew laughed and took them again, hiding them behind his back. 'All you need to see is your board and the shore.'

Caitlin gave in, knowing it was ridiculous to be getting into a tug of war over her glasses. But why was this man determined to treat her as if she were a gauche teenager? She was a grown woman, for God's sake, a respected professional.

'Okay, then,' she said, only too aware that she sounded like a sulky teenager. 'But you might have to lead the way.'

Down on the beach the sun was sinking, turning the clouds candy-floss pink. A small breeze had picked up, forming small caps of white on the previously still water. Again Caitlin wondered what she had let herself in for.

'Stay near the shore,' Andrew ordered while he rigged the child-sized windsurfer. 'If by any chance, and I think it's unlikely, you manage to get on your feet and stay upright, don't panic.

If you feel you're been carried out to sea, just let the sail go, sit on the board and I'll come and get you in the rescue boat.'

His words made Caitlin determined. Come hell or high water, she'd get upright and stay upright. She would show him in the same way she had shown her brothers every time they had told her she couldn't do something because she was a girl. Finally once the board was rigged and Andrew had given her instructions about how to hold the sail, he retrieved a lifejacket from the speedboat, slipped it over her arms and fastened the straps around her waist. Once more she was uncomfortably aware of him as he bent his head. Her knees began to tremble. Whether it was from fear or his proximity she didn't want to know.

Andrew rolled up his jeans and pushed the board into the water, signalling Caitlin to follow. She splashed after him, pleasantly surprised that even when the water leaked into her suit it was agreeably warm. Her first attempt to pull up the sail ended with her back in the water. Seeing that Andrew was enjoying himself at her expense, she gritted her teeth and jumped back on the board. After another three failed attempts suddenly the board was up and she was off, heading out to sea. She placed her feet on either side of the sail, and put her arms in the bow and arrow position, just as he had shown her. Hey, this isn't so difficult, she thought, not too much different from balancing on a horse, but then, having lost her concentration for a moment, she was back in the water. Looking back to the shore, she was dismayed to find she had only managed a couple of metres. Andrew was watching from the beach, but without her glasses she couldn't read his expression.

Determined to show him, she hauled herself back on the board, pulled the sail out of the water, noting that it was taking all her strength, and set off once more. This time she stayed up and she felt a thrill of exhilaration as she felt the sea race underneath. After a minute or two she began to enjoy herself and played around, moving the sail backwards and forwards, beginning to understand what made the board speed up and what movement slowed it down. But after another few minutes she looked back over her shoulder and was shocked to find that she could no longer see Andrew. If she carried on at this rate, she would be in Timbuctoo before she knew it.

Now, what had he said about turning around and going back? But she couldn't remember. The board continued towards the horizon with Caitlin feeling more horrified with every passing minute. Then she remembered what he had said about letting the sail drop. So she did. And then she was back in the water. She rose to the surface gasping and spluttering, and grabbed hold of the board. Had Andrew said anything about sharks being this far out? She wasn't going to wait to find out. She turned the board around and faced it in the other direction. She discovered it was a lot easier going out than in as she slowly tacked back to shore. She couldn't help but feel a surge of satisfaction as she returned safely towards the beach. Andrew waded in and helped her pull the board up onto the sand.

'Hey, I'm impressed,' he said. 'I was just about to come and get you when you turned around.

Next time I'll show you how to do it without having to fall in the water.'

Caitlin scooped some water in her hands and threw it at him. 'Just a girl, huh?'

Working together, they unfastened the sail from the board. The sun had sunk below the horizon, turning the sky cobalt blue. 'How are we doing for time?' Caitlin asked.

'We've another hour or so,' Andrew replied. 'I didn't expect you to get the hang of it so quickly. You grab a shower, if you like, while I put this away. If you could leave the suit by the door, I'll give it a rinse when I get back.'

Caitlin trudged back to the house, the heavy sand making her legs feel wobbly. For the first time in months, even years, she felt exhilarated by something apart from her work. She was glad that she had allowed Andrew to persuade her to have a go. Maybe it was about time she started taking some time off to learn new skills.

She hesitated outside the door. Andrew had suggested she leave the wetsuit here and she didn't want to trail sand into the house. But she was naked underneath. How would she negotiate the distance to the shower from the door? Looking around, she could see no sign of Andrew. She hopped from foot to foot, but then she noticed a towel had been placed over the rails on the veranda. Peeling off the suit, she dropped it by the door, grabbed the towel and wrapped it around herself. She was just in time to cover her nakedness before Andrew appeared.

'You found it, then?' he said. He leaned against the balcony and watched her from hooded eyes. Caught in his stare like a rabbit in headlights, Caitlin willed her legs to move but she couldn't. It was as if she was frozen. The humid air settled around her as she took a deep breath. Then, before she knew what was happening, she was in Andrew's arms and he was kissing her. She could feel the warmth of his naked chest against her body, the tiny drops of water cooling her overheated skin. Still holding on to the towel with one hand, she melted into his body. His arms curled around her, dropping to her waist as he kissed her with an intensity she had never experienced before. A small voice in her head was telling her to stop, but she pushed it away. The feel of his lips on hers, the pressure of his hands on her lower back as he pressed her hips into his, was too good to resist.

Then suddenly she felt herself lifted as he kicked open the door of the house and carried her towards the bedroom. She snaked her arms around his neck as his kisses grew ever deeper. Everything disappeared around her as she gave in to the delightful sensations that were coursing through her body. All she could think was that she wanted him. Wanted him more than she'd thought it was possible for a woman to want a man.

He laid her on the bed and raised his head. She could read the same urgent need in his eyes, in the curve of his lips, that she felt. He looked at her in a silent question. Her answer was to pull him closer.

Later as she lay in his arms she felt nothing of the embarrassment or awkwardness that—had she given it any thought at all—she would have imagined. Instead, as she ran a finger along the contours of his chest, she felt amazed. Never before had making love felt so right. Although she barely knew this man, she realised she knew everything she needed to.

'Are you hungry?' Andrew asked, tracing the line of her lips with a finger.

'I don't know why, but my appetite seems to have deserted me,' she whispered back.

Andrew jumped out of bed. 'Stay right there,' he ordered. 'Don't you move a muscle.' He returned a little while later with a tray laden with fruit, biscuits and cheese and a bottle of wine. 'I've cancelled the table,' he said. 'But I thought I should feed you up a little. You're going to need your energy later.' He grinned wolfishly as he cut off a piece of Brie and, adding a grape, popped it into Caitlin's mouth. They lay in bed, feeding each other and laughing. Caitlin didn't want to talk about the future, if indeed there was a future. All she wanted right now was to be here in this space that had become her whole world. She didn't want to talk about how she felt. Any admission of love on her part would demand some sort of response from him, and that wasn't the way she wanted it to be.

But deep down in a place she wasn't ready to explore, Caitlin knew that for the first time in her life she had fallen deeply and irrevocably in love and she didn't like it. Not one bit.

CHAPTER SEVEN

WHEN Caitlin woke, the sun was streaming through the window. For a moment she couldn't remember where she was, then it all came flooding back. The night before, Andrew's arms around her, making love. Stretching luxuriously, she turned, only to find the space beside her was empty. From the kitchen the sound of pots and pans clattering assaulted her ears and the smell of freshly brewed coffee filtered tantalisingly up her nostrils.

How had that happened? she wondered. When had she gone from admiring Andrew as a colleague and friend to knowing that she was in love with him? And what was she going to do about it? It was a complication she didn't need in her life right now. His life was here, in Australia, while her future lay in Ireland. She was so close to the position she had worked so hard for all her life, there was no way she was going to give it up now. But, she told herself, it was early days. She still had another few months in Australia, plenty of time to take everything slowly, cautiously—the way she liked her life to happen.

Andrew strode into the room, wearing his jeans and nothing else. Immediately Caitlin felt another surge of desire that left her breathless. This taking things slowly wasn't going to be easy, she thought, not when all she wanted right now was a repeat of last night. In fact, she admitted ruefully, all she wanted was to stay here, in this room with Andrew, and shut the rest of the world out.

'G'day,' Andrew said, smiling down at her. 'I brought you some breakfast.' Caitlin eyed the soggy toast warily and shook her head. 'Coffee is fine for now,' she said.

At Andrew's look of disappointment she almost laughed out loud. 'All right,' she relented. 'Just a bite or two.' She bit into the toast, which tasted as bad as she expected. Clearly, whatever talents Andrew had, cooking wasn't one of them.

'You've got a crumb,' Andrew said, touching the corner of her mouth. 'Just there.' His fingers traced the corner of her mouth then dropped to her jaw. Caitlin felt heat low in her belly as his finger continued over her neck and down to her breasts. He lifted the tray away and dropped his lips to follow the path of his fingers. Caitlin took a sharp intake of breath as he dropped kisses as tender as raindrops ever downwards. She arched her back and raked her nails across his back, pulling him closer. As he lay alongside her she felt his responding desire. She tugged at the button of his jeans, dipping her hands below the waistband. Andrew raised himself on one elbow and looked deep into her eyes. 'Say it,' he demanded, his eyes black with desire.

'I want you,' she whispered. 'Now. Please.'

Much later they lay naked and hot in each other's arms, the sheet entangled in their limbs. Outside Caitlin could hear the crash of the waves on the shore and a gentle breeze cooled her skin. She laid her head on his chest, listening to the steady beat of his heart. Andrew stroked her hair.

'Lunch?' he questioned softly. Whatever was happening between them lay unspoken, almost as if neither of them wanted to break the spell. Did Andrew feel the same way she did? Caitlin wondered. If so, what next? But the never-far-away sensible voice was hovering on the edges of her mind. *Don't think about it, just do what everyone has been telling you to do. Live for the moment and let the future take care of itself.*

She lifted her head and looked into serious brown eyes. It was a different side to Andrew she was seeing. He too looked as if he had been taken by surprise.

'Can we stay here?' Caitlin asked. She wasn't sure she was ready to return to the everyday world. Not now, maybe tomorrow or the next day. At some point she'd have to think about the future but for now it could wait.

'We have all weekend,' Andrew said. 'We don't need to go back until tomorrow evening. I'm happy to stay in bed until then, although I have to warn you, I need to eat some time. In the meantime phone Brianna and let her know that you won't be back until tomorrow.'

Caitlin phoned a distinctly curious Brianna and mumbled some excuse about Andrew wanting to show her something or another. It was clear that Brianna wasn't fooled for a moment.

'What's going on? You and Andrew haven't… God, you have, haven't you? Cat, please be careful. You're not used to men like him.'

'Hey, Bri, I'm old enough to look after myself. Anyway, you told me to get a life and have some fun, and that's what I'm doing.' But even as she was saying the words, Caitlin knew it was far more than that. 'He's teaching me to windsurf and then…' inspiration hit her '…I'm taking him horse riding after lunch.'

'Horse riding? But I don't think Andrew rides. In fact, I'm pretty sure he won't go near them. I suggested it once and he was horrified. Refused point blank.'

'If I can have a go at windsurfing then he'll have to do what I want,' Caitlin said. She had promised to pay him back and this would be a perfect way to do it. 'I'm going to find some-where.' Her sister coughed. Instantly Caitlin was on the alert. 'Are you feeling okay, Bri?'

'What did I tell you about not fussing?' her sister said. 'I'm fine, Niall's fine and the kids are great. We're going down to the beach later, and to the botanic gardens tomorrow. Niall has to go away again on business on Monday morning, so we want to make the most of the weekend with the kids. Hold on a minute, Niall's saying something.' Caitlin hung on, listening to the mumble of voices. Out of the corner of her eye she saw Andrew gesticulating that he was going for a shower. Then Brianna came back on the phone. 'Niall says could you tell Andrew that he'll be seeing his parents while he's in Sydney. Does he have a message?'

'Hang on a minute until I ask him,' Caitlin said. She passed the message on to Andrew.

'Ask Niall to tell them I'm looking forward to seeing them in a couple of weeks' time,' Andrew replied. 'And say hi to everyone.'

Caitlin did as he requested. By the time she replaced the receiver she could hear the sound of water running. Andrew was going to Sydney soon, then. Caitlin felt her heart dip. How long for? she wondered. She knew however long he would be away she would miss him. It seemed that taking this—whatever it was—casually wasn't going to be quite as easy as she had hoped. She didn't know the rules of a love affair any more. She had met David soon after finishing medical school and their romance had been a slow, considered one. It was only after being together for four years that they had agreed to live together and had spent the next few years in what Caitlin now recognised as palid domesticity. They had talked about marriage, but neither had ever quite taken up the gauntlet. She had loved David, but now she realised it had been the love of one friend for another. She had never felt an iota of the pulse-racing roller-coaster feelings she was experiencing even just thinking about Andrew. She didn't know the rules, she realised. She was already in much deeper than she had ever imagined possible.

Andrew took her down to the restaurant where they had planned to eat the night before. While he was in the shower, Caitlin had arranged a horse-riding trip to a waterhole, assuring the owner of the stables that she had been brought up with horses and they wouldn't need a guide.

She studied Andrew surreptitiously while he perused the menu. Dressed in clean jeans and a T-shirt that showed off his muscular arms, he looked calm and relaxed. She, on the other hand, felt anything but. She desperately wanted him to say something, anything, that might tell her how he felt. She was damned if she was going to be the first to say anything. If the weekend was a one-off, she would have to deal with it when the time came.

'You have to try the Moreton Bay bugs,' Andrew said. 'I never have anything else when I come here.'

'It sounds revolting,' Caitlin said, screwing up her nose. 'Who on earth would want to eat bugs?'

'I thought you were going to try being more adventurous?' he teased. 'Anyway, they're not bugs. They're more like lobster. Trust me?' As she looked into his warm brown eyes, Caitlin wondered if there was a hidden meaning to his words. Did she trust him? As a doctor, yes. As a friend, yes. With her heart? Not really, she admitted sadly.

'Okay,' she said. 'But I have a surprise, well, more like a challenge for you.' She waited until Andrew had given the order to the waiter, before continuing. 'I've arranged for us to go horse-back riding this afternoon.' Seeing that Andrew was about to protest, she held up a restraining hand. 'So far, I have done everything you have asked. I think it's only fair that you do some-thing you're not quite comfortable with.'

He smiled wryly. 'Okay. Can't have you going back to Ireland and saying Aussie men chicken out. I hate the brutes, but if that's what you want, I'll give it a go.'

The lunch when it arrived was every bit as de-licious as Andrew had promised. So far, she had gone against her instincts to stay safe, and had been rewarded. She only hoped that taking a risk with Andrew wasn't going to be the one that undid her. As they ate they chatted about work.

'Brianna tells me you're some big shot in Ireland,' Andrew said.

'I suppose that's one way of putting it.' Caitlin laughed. 'I have done a lot of research into in-fertility, which seems to have caught the imagination internationally. It's also gone a long way to raising funds for the university we're affiliated to, and there's talk about offering me a chair on my return.' Although she tried, Caitlin couldn't help the note of pride creeping into her voice. But why not? She had worked hard for her success.

'Good for you,' Andrew said. Although his tone seemed genuinely warm, something shifted in his eyes. 'Seems to me you have your life all mapped out. Career-wise anyway. What about the rest of it. Marriage at least, if not kids?'

Caitlin felt cold fingers of dread wrap around her heart. 'I haven't really thought about it. I was with someone for a few years, someone who works in the same department as me. Neither marriage nor children was really on the agenda back then. We were—are—both too focussed on our careers.' Andrew eyebrows puckered.

'As far as marriage is concerned, if the right man came along, that would be great, as long as he understood how important my career was. And as for kids…' She chewed on her lip. 'Like I said to you before, I don't know if they figure in my plans. Besides, if I get the chair, I'll need to commit myself to the job for a few years before I could even consider maternity leave.'

'What, you'd go back to work after having children? Do you think that's right?'

'Look, it's unlikely I'll have children but *if* I ever do,' Caitlin stressed, 'then, sure, I'd go back to work. I haven't worked this hard and this long to throw it all away.' Andrew narrowed his eyes at her.

'You think that's fair? To have someone else raise your children? Why have them?'

Caitlin was aghast at the turn the conversation was taking. How had they got into this? 'Andrew, loads of women have children and work. It's more the norm than not.'

'I don't accept that,' he said. 'As soon as my parents married my mother stayed at home to look after the house and the family. She never regretted it. It's the right thing to do.'

Caitlin wasn't sure she was hearing correctly. This was a different, totally unexpected side to Andrew. One she couldn't quite reconcile with the man she thought she was beginning to know.

Andrew had never struck her as anything except a modern Australian man.

'My mother was a stay-at-home wife and mother until we left home,' Caitlin said slowly. 'And with five children to bring up, I don't blame her. But I was always aware of how hard she worked. She trained to be a nurse, you know, but she never used her training. I know she always regretted not following her dream, although I also know she loves us and Dad more than anything. It was her who brought me up to believe I should have a career, make something of my life.'

'And you don't think bringing up children is making something of your life?' Andrew argued. 'The most important job of all.'

'I can see we're not going to agree,' Caitlin said quietly. 'Maybe we should change the subject?' But the day had lost its sparkle. Caitlin was only too aware of how different she and Andrew were. Miles apart, in fact. She could never be the type of woman he wanted, and it seemed that he wasn't the sort of man she could ever imagine herself sharing her life with.

* * *

After lunch, Andrew called for the bill and insisted on paying. 'Let me pay half,' Caitlin suggested, but one look at the set of his jaw made her back down. It had simply not occurred to her, as masculine as Andrew was, that he was so conventional when it came to gender roles.

'Do you want to forget about the horse riding?' she asked. 'Go back to Brisbane instead?' How could she have been so stupid? This was exactly what happened when you threw caution to the wind. Now she had gone and fallen for a man from whom it seemed she was miles apart.

'Hell, no,' Andrew said, the stormclouds clearing from his face. 'And having you tell everyone I chickened out? Not on your life.'

Caitlin couldn't help a small shiver of satisfaction when she saw Andrew blanch at the size of his horse. Staying resolutely in role, he said nothing, but whistled nonchalantly. But Caitlin wasn't deceived. For the first time since she had met him she was seeing an Andrew Bedi well out of his comfort zone. That would teach him to be so macho all the time.

'You can still change your mind,' she said as he climbed into the saddle. His horse, sensing his discomfort, reared and Caitlin had to lean forward to catch the reins before he bolted with Andrew.

'Let's just get on with it,' Andrew replied through gritted teeth. Caitlin gave him a quick lesson on how to hold the reins and what to do with the stirrups, relishing the opportunity to turn the tables on him. Thankfully for Andrew, the stables had supplied them with American-style saddles that, given their depth, would offer Andrew a little more security. He shifted around in the saddle before leaning towards Caitlin and asking in a whisper, 'What am I supposed to do about…you know?' Caitlin followed his glance downwards and grinned.

'Not a lot you can do, I'm afraid. Just one of those things men have to put up with.' They headed off at a walk, the owner having explained where to go to find the waterhole. As soon as they were out of sight, Caitlin suggested they try a canter. 'You'll probably find it easier than a trot,' she explained. 'Especially on the you-know-whats.'

'Let's get this over with,' Andrew replied through gritted teeth.

Caitlin kicked her horse into a canter, turning around in the saddle to see how Andrew was doing. Unfortunately he was bouncing around like a sack of potatoes, holding on to the reins as if his life depended on it. Trying not to laugh, Caitlin yelled, 'Relax, Andrew. Just go with the movement,' before kicking her horse on.

When she next risked a backward glance she was surprised to see that Andrew was beginning to get the hang of it. He was moving more comfortably with the horse and had loosened his grip on the reins.

Half an hour later they found the watering hole and Caitlin dismounted and waited for Andrew to catch up. The sun was still high in the sky and that, combined with the exercise, had left Caitlin with a sheen of sweat covering her body.

As Andrew came to an undignified stop, she gathered the reins of his horse and tied them to a tree close to hers.

'I don't think I'm going to be able to walk for days,' he groaned. 'Or do anything else for that matter.' He slid her a devilish grin.

'Is there anything likely to be lurking in there?' Caitlin pointed to the pool of aquamarine water.

'No, I think it's pretty safe,' Andrew said, slipping off his T-shirt. 'But even crocs won't keep me out.' His jeans and boxers followed the T-shirt and then he was in the water. 'Come on in,' he called. 'It's great.' And then he disappeared from view as he submerged his head in the murky water.

Caitlin stood confused. Since their discussion over lunch, she had resolutely refused to think about the significance of Andrew's words. But could she really act as if they had meant nothing? Perhaps now was the time to speak to him, before she got in any deeper. But before she had the time to formulate her words, Andrew strode out of the water and picked her up in his arms. Ignoring her squeals of protest, he removed her glasses and baseball cap, placing them a safe distance from the horses, and carried her, fully dressed, into the cool water. Caitlin gasped as the water seeped over her skin, soaking her shorts and T-shirt. But he was right. It was a delicious relief.

As she gasped from the shock of the water on her overheated skin, he brought his mouth down on hers. Despite her reservations of only moments before, she responded hungrily, drawing him closer and kissing him back with all the pent-up passion of the last few years. *Just let me have this time. I'll be sensible later*, was her last coherent thought as Andrew carried her out of the pool and placed her on a bed of leaves. Then they were both pulling at her clothes, urgent in their need. As Andrew's face swam before her, Caitlin once more was powerless to prevent herself giving in to him.

Later, they unpacked the provisions the owner of the stables had provided and Andrew showed her how to brew tea in a billy can while they munched on fruit and fresh bread. Caitlin watched as he worked, relishing the look of his bronze skin and the way his muscles rippled as he moved. As she picked leaves out of her hair that lay in a mass of tangles around her shoulders, she wondered where the cool, calm, collected Dr O'Neill of only a couple of weeks ago had disappeared to. She knew that that woman was gone for ever, but who had replaced her? Certainly not the woman Andrew had described earlier.

As they sipped their tea, Caitlin made up her mind. Regardless of the change in her, she was still a woman who needed to know what lay ahead. She couldn't pretend to herself, no matter how much she wanted to, that she was able to continue with a relationship, no matter how heady, under false pretences. But still she hesitated, knowing somewhere deep in her soul that once she spoke, things would never be the same between them again.

'Tell me about your family,' she said, trying to ease her way into the conversation.

'Not much to tell,' he said. 'Parents are first-generation Australians, came over here just after they got married and have worked incredibly hard to build a successful business.'

'I thought your mother didn't work.'

'She worked to support my father by looking after the home and the children.'

'Children?' Caitlin queried, feeling slightly guilty as she already knew the answer from what Brianna had told her. But she wanted to hear Andrew's story from his own lips. Perhaps it would offer another glimpse of the real Dr Bedi. 'I thought you were an only child?'

Andrew rose to his feet and, keeping his back to her, spoke softly. 'I had a sister, an older sister.'

'Had?' Caitlin prompted.

'She died following a post-partum haemorrhage. The baby died too,' Andrew said curtly.

'I am so sorry.' Caitlin came to stand behind him, wrapping her arms around his waist and leaning her head against his back.

'It was ten years ago,' Andrew said. 'I still miss her.'

'Did she leave any other children?'

'No. It's only me left.' He laughed shortly. 'I'm my parents' whole world now. They depend on me for their future—to carry on the family line.'

'What do you mean?' Caitlin asked, prompted at the strange emphasis he gave the words.

'They hope I'll meet someone—someone

from the same background—who will have the same values as we do.'

'Are you telling me that you are considering an arranged marriage? That your parents want you to marry an Indian girl?' Caitlin asked, feeling a cool breeze run through her soul.

'It would make them very happy,' he said. 'But it wouldn't be an arranged marriage as such. I couldn't ever marry someone I didn't like and admire. Not even to keep my parents happy. But you should know, Caitlin, that this isn't something my parents are forcing on me. While I do have a duty to them, I happen to truly believe that Western marriages are more likely to fail than Indian ones, precisely because they aren't built on mutual respect and common values.'

Caitlin was reeling from Andrew's revelations. But hadn't she, until recently, thought the same thing? That the best marriages were based on respect and affection rather than passion, which would inevitably pass with time? And why was she now so certain that she had been wrong? She knew now, with absolute certainty, that she could never marry anyone she wasn't totally, desperately, head over heels in love with. The way she loved Andrew.

'What does that mean for us?' she said softly, willing her voice to remain steady.

Andrew turned and looked at Caitlin, holding her away so he could look directly into her eyes.

'Us?' he echoed. 'I'm sorry, Caitlin, I hadn't really thought about an us. You are a beautiful, exceptional woman, a woman who I want to spend time with, but…'

'But…' Caitlin repeated, feeling chilled to the bone.

'We have different ambitions, goals in life. You want your career—you've made that very clear, and you should be proud of yourself that you are so successful. But as for me, I want my career and eventually, not for years yet, to find someone my parents approve of, who will want the same things in life that I do. We both want different things from our futures. In the meantime, can't we just enjoy what we have? Make the most of our time together?'

She turned away from him, lest he see the disappointment in her eyes. 'I'm sorry, Andrew. I know it's late in the day, and I suppose you could say I came into this with my eyes wide open, but I'm not the sort of woman who can take a relationship casually. Just for sex. That, I suppose, is the main difference between you and me.'

He grabbed her arm and turned her back to face him. 'What are you saying, Caitlin?'

'I'm saying, Andrew, that as much as I've enjoyed this time with you, it's over.' The words sounded formal and stiff, but Caitlin was finding it difficult to speak through the tightness in her throat. If this weekend had meant anything to him, and from the way he had held her, made love to her, she couldn't believe it hadn't, then he'd be willing to try and meet her halfway. But, then, she reminded herself, she really didn't know how men thought.

He gave her one last searching look and then dropped his arms in defeat. 'You're right,' he said. 'I have been a selfish idiot.'

Unspeakably disappointed at how easily he was giving her up, Caitlin tried a smile. If he felt so little for her, she was damned if she was going to let him see how much he had hurt her.

'I think we should go now,' she said quietly. 'I'd like to get back to Brisbane tonight, preferably before it's dark.'

'Caitlin.' He reached out towards her and touched her hair. For a second Caitlin thought he was going to say something that would make this whole horrible mess all right. But instead he stepped away from her. 'We'd better get going,' he said.

The journey back to Brisbane was a quiet affair, both of them preoccupied with their thoughts. They had stopped at Andrew's beach house to collect their belongings and freshen up, but the light had gone out of the day. Caitlin was relieved when they pulled up outside her sister's house. In the fading light, Caitlin could see that no one was home and she was glad that she wouldn't have to face her sister's questions about her early return until later. Her stomach was churning and she felt mildly nauseous.

'Thank you,' she said stiffly as Andrew handed her her bag. 'I'll see you on Monday.'

'Sure. And, Caitlin, I'm not sorry we had this time together.' He looked at her for a long moment.

'Don't worry, Andrew, I won't let it affect our professional relationship. I'm as much to…' She searched for the right word. 'Blame for what happened as you,' Caitlin said. Then, before she lost all self-control, she bolted inside. She only just made it to the bathroom before she was sick.

'Hey, we didn't expect you until tomorrow,' Brianna said predictably when she found Caitlin wrapped in her dressing gown on the front veranda. She looked at her sister quizzically. 'You don't look great. Are you all right?'

'I think I've picked up a tummy bug,' Caitlin said. And if it was only part of the truth, Caitlin wasn't lying. She had felt dreadfully ill and had been sick twice since her return home.

'Up to bed with you,' Brianna said firmly. 'I'll bring you some peppermint tea. You can tell me all about it tomorrow when you feel better.' Reluctantly, Caitlin let her sister propel her upstairs, dismally aware that it was she who should be looking after Brianna, not the other way round.

When she brought up the tea, she sat on the edge of the bed looking concerned. 'Should I ring someone? Andrew perhaps?'

Caitlin was horrified at the thought. 'It's probably only a twenty-four-hour thing. Plenty of fluids and bed rest is what any doctor would recommend. Honestly, Bri, I'm fine. But how are you?'

'We had a lovely day,' Brianna said. 'It's funny how being ill can make you appreciate all the little things. Every day is special.'

'You're not worried, Bri? You're feeling okay?' Caitlin sat up, almost knocking over her tea in the process. 'You've not felt any new lumps, have you? You're looking a little flushed to me. And I can hear you still have that cough.'

'Caitlin,' Bri said warningly, 'you're fussing again. I'm probably a bit flushed because I caught the sun. And as for the cough, it's hardly more than a tickle. It's just that I have my check-up this week and I guess I'm just feeling a bit ansty, wondering if they'll be recommending more treatment. I wish Niall wasn't going to be in Sydney so he could come with me for moral support.'

'I didn't know your check-up was this week. I'll come with you.'

'What about the hospital? I'm sure they won't be keen on you having time off so soon after you've started. Really, Cat, I'm just being silly, I'll be fine on my own. I know how much you hate missing work.'

Caitlin was shocked that her sister would think, even for a moment, that she'd put work ahead of her. But, then, Caitlin admitted ruefully, all Brianna had ever known of her sister was this work-obsessed dervish, who rarely had time for anything else. Was that how everyone saw her? Someone who couldn't imagine a life without work?

'I'm coming with you and that's that,' Caitlin said firmly.

Brianna leaned across and gave her a hug. Again Caitlin was dismayed at how fragile her sister felt. She was so strong willed, so determined and upbeat, it was easy to forget how much her illness had taken out of her. 'Thank you, love. It means a lot to me.' She lifted the empty teacup from the side of the bed. 'You get some sleep now, if you want to be fit for work on Monday.'

'Bri,' Caitlin whispered just before her sister left the room, 'I'm sorry, if I haven't been a very good sister to you. You know I love you.'

Brianna's smile lit up the room. 'Of course, you idiot, and I love you too. Now, go to sleep.' And she turned out the light, leaving Caitlin to her dismal thoughts.

Andrew let himself into his flat and threw the car keys down on the sideboard. Feeling restless, he contemplated going for a walk, then discarded the idea and switched on the television to watch the news. But it was no use. He couldn't concentrate on the flickering images in front of him. Instead the image of green eyes and red hair kept intruding on his thoughts. He hadn't meant to make love to Caitlin—it had just happened and when it had it had felt so natural. The memory of holding her in his arms, the feel of her satin skin against his, made him groan aloud. He had been attracted to Caitlin from the moment he had pulled her from the water. He smiled as he remembered the set of her mouth as she had tried to hold on to her dignity, the way that she had slowly melted in his arms and the flash of temper whenever she thought herself thwarted. He had loved watching her change from the almost uptight woman with every hair in place to the passionate, fiery, laughing woman whom he had held in his arms. But what had he been thinking? If he had been thinking at all.

He stood and went over to the window, looking out over the lights of the city. Caitlin O'Neill wasn't the sort of woman a man treated lightly. But neither was she the woman he could see himself spending the rest of his life with. He could never be satisfied with a woman who didn't put him and their children first. He admired her as a doctor, of course he did. What was there not to admire in her clinical skills and her obvious empathy for her patients? But…and this was the part he couldn't accept…Caitlin was the sort of woman who would want life on her terms. And it was beginning to dawn on Andrew that perhaps he had met his match in Dr Caitlin O'Neill. She wasn't the kind of woman a man could forget easily. In fact, he realised, as he thought of never holding her again, she was the sort of woman a man couldn't forget at all.

CHAPTER EIGHT

'COME in and have a seat,' the oncologist, a tired-looking woman in her late forties, welcomed Brianna and Caitlin.

'This is my sister, Dr Caitlin O'Neill, Antonia. Caitlin, Dr Antonia Sommerville.'

'I've heard of you,' Antonia said, looking over her bifocals. 'You're the whiz kid obstetrician from Ireland. I hadn't made the connection, I'm afraid.'

'Hardly a kid.' Caitlin laughed.

'But very young to have got where you are all the same,' Antonia said. Then she turned intelligent brown eyes on Brianna.

'My secretary is just rustling up your results. I gather the nurses took some blood from you earlier. We'll just wait until they arrive, but how have you been?' All at once the severe expression was replaced by a look of genuine concern. 'Kids letting you rest?'

'You know kids.' Brianna shrugged. 'But Cat's been a great help.'

Antonia turned her gaze on Caitlin. 'And have you been checked out?' she asked.

'Er, no, not yet,' Caitlin admitted. 'I haven't really had the time.'

'In that case…' Antonia picked up the phone '…I shall arrange for you to be seen at my clinic as soon as they can fit you in.'

Caitlin could only watch open-mouthed as a few minutes later Antonia passed her a slip with an appointment for the following week.

'I know doctors,' she said, smiling grimly, 'being one myself. Unless they are bullied they never quite find the time to look after their own health. Don't you miss it now,' she added, wagging a finger at Caitlin, who suddenly felt six years old. 'These appointments are like gold dust.'

'Okay, Brianna, while we're waiting, why don't you pop up on the table while I examine your breasts?' Just then Caitlin's pager bleeped. She had arranged for one of the other obstetricians to cover her for an hour or two, so was a little surprised.

'You can use the phone on my desk.' Antonia indicated with a nod, before drawing the screen around Brianna.

When the number Caitlin dialled was answered, she was surprised to find Andrew on the other end.

'Oh, hello, Caitlin,' he said, sounding distracted. 'A call has just come through from one of the outlying towns. There's a mother who is in late labour and looks like she'll be needing a section. I'm going to attend, but obviously we need an obstetrician. Would you like to come?'

Caitlin would have loved to go, but it only took her a second to make up her mind. She had promised Brianna she would be with her and unless there was no one else to take the call, here she'd stay.

'Could one of the others go?' she asked. 'Just this once? I'd love to go, but I have something else I really need to do.' With a pang Caitlin realised this was the first time she had ever put something else before her work. She was beginning to realise how much she had missed.

'Sure. Dr Forest is happy to go. He's the obstetrician on call this week so he'd usually be the first choice anyway. There will be other opportunities. Possibly the week you're on call.' He dropped his voice. 'Is everything okay, Cat?'

It was the first time he had used her sister's pet name for her and she felt an irrational tingle of pleasure. 'It's just I'm in Oncology with Brianna for her check-up. I promised I would stay. So if you're sure Dr Forest is happy to go, then please go ahead.'

'Okay,' Andrew replied. 'I've got to go. The air ambulance is taking off in a few minutes. But, Cat, you will let me know that Brianna's okay, won't you?'

'Yes, of course,' Caitlin said, replacing the receiver.

By this time the secretary had put a set of results on the desk. Caitlin was tempted to lean over and check them out while Antonia was occupied with Brianna behind the screens. But she stopped herself. It would be a breach of medical etiquette as well as a betrayal of her sister's privacy.

Instead she waited patiently until Antonia and Brianna returned to their places at the desk. She watched closely as Antonia read the results and when her expression altered Caitlin knew instantly something was wrong. Cold fingers of dread caressed her spine.

Eventually she put the papers down and leaned across to Brianna. 'The good news is that your breasts seem fine. No recurring lumps or bumps as far as I can tell. But I'm afraid your bloods do give me cause for concern. Your white-cell count is very low. I'm not sure exactly why, but I'd like to admit you to hospital for a few days so we can find out.'

Brianna reached for Caitlin's hand, and Caitlin grasped the cold fingers in hers, trying to pass her strength on to her sister.

'Has the cancer come back?' Brianna breathed.

'As I said, I won't know what this means until we run further tests. But with a blood count that low, you run the risk of infection, or already have an infection. You'll be safer in hospital. I know it's difficult, and easy for me to say, but try not to worry until we know more.'

Brianna turned green eyes on Caitlin. 'Cat?' she said, with only the tiniest tremor evident.

Caitlin knew there could be all sorts of reasons for the white blood count being low. Some fairly innocuous, others less so. But she remembered the cough and the flushed look her sister had had the last few days. If she did have an infection it could be very dangerous. She pushed away the fear and strove to keep her voice calm and steady.

'Dr Sommerville is correct. There could be lots of reasons for the count being low. That's what we need to find out. In the meantime, the safest place for you is in hospital.'

'But what about the children?' Brianna asked. Caitlin could see it was taking all her effort not to break down. 'Niall's not due back until the weekend.'

'Don't you think you should phone him and let him know what's happening?' Caitlin said gently. 'I'm sure he'd take the next plane back.'

'I told you before, Caitlin, I want to keep my life as normal as possible for as long as possible. If I called Niall back every time there was the slightest reason, he'd never get any work done. And he's missed too much time on this important project as it is.' She bit her lip. 'Can't you take some time off and look after the children? Just until Friday? They're at school until after two anyway.' She squeezed Caitlin's hand. 'I know it's a lot to ask. Especially when you haven't been here that long.'

Caitlin knew she couldn't refuse her sister. It would take a bit of arranging, but somehow she would have to manage. For the first time in her life, work was going to have to take second place.

'I'll need to have a chat with my colleagues and see what we can work out. But if they can do without me for a few days then, yes, I'll look after the children for you.'

Caitlin sought out her senior colleague as soon as Brianna had left to return home to pack a bag. Antonia had wanted to admit her straight to the ward, but Brianna had been adamant that she didn't want the children coming home from school to find their mother in hospital. From the set of her mouth, Caitlin could see that she was determined. Although most of the time her sister was easygoing, when she had made up her mind about something, there was no dissuading her. Dr Hargreaves was sympathetic and told Caitlin that he and his other colleagues would cover for her for the remainder of the week. The following week would be difficult, though, he warned, as Dr Foster was taking annual leave. 'But if it's at all possible, could you cover the labour ward until Dr Foster gets back with the air ambulance? I have Theatre in a few minutes, and Susan has an outpatient clinic about to start,' he said, naming the fourth colleague to make up their team.

'Of course I'll stay until he returns. I've patients to pass over anyway. Hopefully Brianna will be out before the end of the week, possibly even tomorrow, in which case I'll be back immediately she's fit,' Caitlin told him. 'At the very least her husband will be back from his business trip and able to step in.'

'I won't expect you until next Monday,' Dr

Hargreaves insisted. 'Do what you have to do. We all have lives outside of medicine.'

By the time Caitlin had seen all her patients and passed on their treatment plans, it was after two. She had phoned Brianna and suggested that she bring the children to the hospital with her. To her surprise, Brianna agreed.

'I don't want them thinking that hospitals are big scary places that they have to be kept away from. They know I used to work here and that you and Andrew still do. I think they'll be fine.'

As soon as Dr Foster returned with the air ambulance, he relieved Caitlin. 'We managed to slow down labour long enough to get the patient here,' he told Caitlin. 'Dr Hargreaves is going to do the section now, before the remainder of his list. He explained to me about your sister, so off you go.'

Caitlin smiled gratefully before giving him a rapid summary of the patients who might need his attention. 'The nurse in charge knows exactly what's going on, if I've left anything out,' she said, before leaving the maternity wing and heading for Oncology.

* * *

Caitlin found Brianna in bed in the ward. A nurse was taking blood.

'Where are the children?' Caitlin asked.

'Andrew's taken them to the canteen for a drink,' Brianna replied. 'He came to see me as soon as he heard I had been admitted.'

'I'd better go and relieve him, then,' Caitlin said, trying to look unconcerned. She would much rather have hung about with Brianna until the test results came back, but she knew that Andrew would need to get on with his own day, and that the children wouldn't be allowed on the ward. 'I'll phone later and see how you're getting on.' Before she left she leaned over and kissed her sister. 'Are you all right?'

'I'm scared,' Brianna admitted. 'What if the cancer's back? What will happen to Niall and the kids?'

It was the first time Caitlin had heard her sister admit her fears and it worried her. Maybe she should phone Niall after all? But she had promised Brianna. No, she would wait for the test results to come back. It would be time enough to make a decision once they knew what they were dealing with.

'But whatever happens, I've decided to have myself tested for the gene. I don't want Siobhan to go through life wondering if and when she is going to be hit with breast cancer.'

'You must do whatever you think is right,' Caitlin said. 'You know I'll support you.'

'Even if it means facing up to the fact you too might have the gene?'

'Yes,' Caitlin said. 'But we'll cross that bridge if and when we have to.' She leaned over and gave her sister a hug.

'I hate to leave you here on your own,' she said.

'At least you're in the same country this time.' Brianna managed a shaky smile. 'And able to be with the children. Besides, Andrew said he'd look in later. Speaking of which, hadn't you better rescue him?'

Caitlin found Siobhan and Ciaran in the canteen. Andrew was saying something to them that made them laugh. As she looked at the three familiar heads, she felt her heart constrict. She wouldn't let herself think of the possibility of the children being left without a mother. That wasn't going to happen. She wouldn't allow it.

Andrew looked up and saw her standing there. With a quiet word to the children he strode across to Caitlin. He put his hand on her shoulder and gave it a gentle squeeze.

'I'll go and check up on Bri later, and I'll call round on my way home and bring you up to speed.'

Caitlin was grateful he didn't offer any of the usual platitudes. There was no point in him telling her not to worry. He seemed to know instinctively what she needed from him.

Caitlin spent the rest of the afternoon in the pool with the children. Then it was time for their homework while she made supper. After that it was bathtime. The children were playing up a little, the change of routine obviously unsettling them. But Caitlin eventually persuaded them out of the bath and into their pyjamas. Somehow she had managed to get herself soaked to the skin, and was beginning to wonder how she'd manage the next few days. Just as she'd tucked them into bed and reached for the storybook they wanted, she heard Andrew's car pull up at the door. Although she desperately wanted to find out about Bri, she decided it would be better to wait until the children had gone to sleep.

'Hey,' Andrew said from the door of the children's bedroom. Before Caitlin could stop them the children had leapt out of bed and straight into Andrew's arms. He picked one under each arm and strode back to their beds.

'It's bedtime, guys,' he said firmly. He looked over at Caitlin. She must look a sight, she thought, dismally aware of her wet clothes and that her hair was all over the place. 'Why don't I read you the story while Aunty Cat puts her feet up?'

Caitlin opened her mouth to protest. Despite appearances, she was coping just fine. How dared he suggest that she was less than capable? On the other hand, it had been an exhausting afternoon and, she conceded reluctantly, Andrew seemed to have a natural calming effect on the children. Instead, she smiled her gratitude at him. A change of clothes before she heard about Bri wouldn't be a bad idea. At the bedroom door, she glanced back at the children but already they were cuddled up to Andrew, one on each side, as he read them a story. Her heart twisted. He'd make such a good father one day, she thought. Caitlin sighed inwardly. Another reason why they weren't right for each other, she reminded herself.

Having changed into dry jeans and a T-shirt, Caitlin telephoned the hospital. But the news had been inconclusive—Brianna was to stay in for a few more days yet until the doctors had got all the results back. Which Caitlin knew was perfectly reasonable—from a professional point of view. So why was she feeling so unsettled and fretful about Brianna? She was the cool-headed one—wasn't she? Sighing, Caitlin made her way out to the veranda. The sun had set and the sky was dotted with a thousand stars. In the distance, she could hear the gentle sound of the waves crashing softly onto the beach. But instead of feeling relaxed, her stomach was taut with nerves.

She sensed Andrew's presence and turned around.

'Fast asleep, both of them,' he said softly. As he eased himself into the chair opposite, his eyes held hers. 'And how are you doing?'

Caitlin swallowed hard to hide the swirl of emotions inside her, caused not only by her concern for her sister but also his presence, if the truth were known.

'I'm fine! Really.' She forced herself to keep her tone even. 'Just worried about Brianna. I phoned the hospital but there's no news. Just that she's settled and sleeping.'

'I know you must be worried about Brianna. It's only natural.'

'Brianna's going to be fine,' she replied firmly, but without warning her throat tightened up and tears that she had been unaware of suddenly threatened to spill. Horrified, Caitlin wiped them away with the back of her hand, not wanting Andrew to see. But it was too late. In one movement he was up and had crossed over to her. He took her in his arms, as she leant into him. She felt safe and secure, and the tears flowed in earnest. 'I'm sorry,' she choked into his chest. 'I'm overtired.'

'Shh,' he said. 'Just let go. For once. You're entitled to be upset. She's your sister, for God's sake.' Caitlin allowed herself a moment, but then pulled away.

Caitlin shook her head in frustration. 'The professional side of me knows that it's probably nothing more sinister than an infection. Horrible as that is, it's treatable. Besides, Brianna needs me to be strong for the kids—and for her.' She blew her nose, mortified that he had seen her blubbing like a baby. Instead, to her surprise, Andrew leaned across and took her hand and wrapped it in his.

'And who is strong for you? Who do you turn to? Because we all need someone to lean on from time to time—even you, Caitlin.' He said the words softly and she could feel the tears threaten to fall again.

Caitlin tried to pull her hand away, but he held on firmly. 'I don't need someone to lean on— I'm not the one going through what Brianna's going through. I can't imagine the fear and uncertainty she must be feeling—especially when it comes to Siobhan and Ciaran, not to mention Niall. And even though I'm a doctor, I can't do one damn thing to help my sister medically.' She breathed deeply, trying to get her emotions back in check. 'So the very least I can do is keep myself together for her and her family. It's what my sister expects of me.'

'You're doing your sister an injustice if you think that. You know as well as I do how a serious illness affects not only the patient but all their loved ones too. The patient has the symptoms, but everyone around them is fighting and coping with the disease too. And just because you're a doctor, it doesn't mean that you have to be in control all the time.'

'I know. I *know* that.' Caitlin wished he would stop being so sympathetic and understanding and so…near. But, she realised suddenly, it felt so good to be able to talk about Brianna's illness with someone. Her mother had been here and her dad had refused to talk about it—as if by not mentioning the word 'cancer', it didn't exist. As for her brothers and sisters, they all looked to her for support and reassurance, even though she was the youngest. She was always the sensible, together sibling of the family. She looked up at Andrew, her eyes large in her face. 'Sometimes I'm so…' Caitlin hesitated, almost unable to bring herself to say the word.

'Scared?' Andrew finished for her.

Caitlin nodded. 'Terrified.' She sucked in her breath. 'Not only for myself if anything happened to my sister, but for her children and her husband. How would they cope? Never mind my parents and the rest of the family. It just doesn't bear thinking about, but sometimes I can't help it. Ridiculous, I know, because so far her treatment has gone well and we owe it to her to be as positive as she is.'

Andrew traced his thumb gently down her cheek, wiping the tears away. 'It's going to be all right, I promise you.'

Although Caitlin knew that he was only trying to reassure her, she was grateful for the words of comfort. For the first time in her life she wished she could draw on the comfort of someone else. Someone like Andrew. Whatever life had to throw at her, she could face it with him at her side. But there was no use thinking like that. He had made it perfectly clear she wasn't the woman he wanted. Whatever she thought she saw in his eyes, she was mistaken. She and Andrew could only ever be friends. She would have to make do with that. Not for the first time, she envied Brianna. However terrible and frightening her life was right now, she had Niall to share her fears with. She would never experience the loneliness that had become a permanent feature in her own life almost without her realising.

The crunch of car tyres on gravel interrupted her thoughts. Caitlin jumped up and looked out of the window. Against the dark she could make out the contours of Niall's car. He must have finished his business early and hoped to surprise Brianna. 'Oh my God, Niall's come home early—he can't see me in such a state. He'll think something really terrible has happened. What am I going to tell him?'

'I called him,' Andrew said calmly. 'I know Brianna didn't want me to, but Niall's a good mate and I know he would never forgive me if I didn't let him know his wife needed him. Sometimes we have to go against the decisions of our friends.'

For a second, Caitlin was furious. How dared he think he knew better than her what was right for Brianna? But just as quickly she knew he was right. Brianna was trying to protect Niall, but Caitlin knew her brother-in-law well enough to know that he'd never forgive himself if something happened to his beloved wife and he wasn't there. How was it that Andrew's intuition as far as her family was concerned was better than hers? She had spent so long cocooned away from real life it seemed as if she had forgotten how to behave.

'Would you mind meeting him and bringing him up to speed while I go to the bathroom to freshen up?' she said. 'Seeing me like this will only scare him half to death.'

CHAPTER NINE

BY THE time Caitlin joined the men in the kitchen, she had got herself back under control again. She kissed her brother-in-law on the cheek and the three of them sat round the kitchen table, discussing Brianna's condition. Niall had gone straight to the hospital from the airport and had little to add to what the nurses had told Caitlin except that Brianna, after her initial annoyance with Andrew, had been delighted that Niall had come.

'She says to tell you she's going to chew your ear off when she next sees you,' Niall told Andrew. Then he turned to Caitlin. 'She was relieved it wasn't you who had told me. She says to tell you she needs someone she can trust not to betray her.'

They discussed Brianna for the next half hour, but there was little either of them could say to really reassure Niall. He looked haggard, Caitlin thought. She could only imagine the toll the last few months had taken on him. What would it be like to be loved the way Niall loved Brianna? she wondered. It seemed to Caitlin as if Niall was doing his best to pretend he believed their optimistic forecast, but she wondered if Niall was doing much the same as she was, hiding his emotions and fears behind a mask of normality. She glanced over at Andrew—perhaps he had comforted his friend in private, the way he had done with her this evening? Despite herself, she felt a rush of affection and gratitude towards Andrew. He had so many layers to him—it was a pity that she would never get to know them all. Because what an intriguing journey that would make!

Eventually Niall changed the subject. 'Had a lovely visit with your folks in Sydney, Andrew. Guess who was there at the same time? Raffia— the beautiful daughter of your dad's business partner. You didn't tell me she's got brains to boot—a mathematician no less!' Niall winked. 'No wonder you've been keeping her a closely guarded secret, you sly devil.'

Andrew laughed shortly, holding up his hands.

'I've been doing nothing of the sort, mate. It's nothing to do with me. It's our parents who want us to meet.' He glanced over at Caitlin, looking uncomfortable. 'We'll see what happens from there. Maybe she won't like what she sees.'

'As if she wouldn't—a fine specimen of a man like yourself?' Niall nudged Caitlin. 'What do you think? Don't you agree, Caitlin? She'll be swooning at his feet.'

Caitlin fought the urge to stalk out the room, horrified that the thought of Andrew holding another woman in his arms filled her with bleak despair. She forced herself to smile. 'What woman wouldn't?' she replied lightly, hoping the two men couldn't hear the irony in her voice. But their words had brought her to her senses. Once her time in Australia was up, and Brianna was well again, she would be going back to Ireland. And to her old life, where she belonged.

Thankfully, Caitlin's initial instincts and diagnosis had been right and with a short dose of IV antibiotics Brianna was discharged home from hospital after a couple of days. Once again, life returned to its normal routine, although Brianna was still weak. Caitlin worked a full day, then rushed home to help with the children. After they were in bed, Brianna usually went too, leaving an exhausted Caitlin to drag herself off to bed.

At the end of the week, reassured that he was no longer needed, Andrew left on his two-week holiday to see his folks in Sydney. Caitlin missed seeing him around the hospital and couldn't stop herself from thinking about him down in Sydney with the gorgeous mathematician. No doubt he'd be wining and dining her and checking out her credentials as a possible mother of his children, she thought bitterly, before reminding herself for the umpteenth time that that was exactly why he was wrong for her. However, as the days passed, she couldn't stop her heart skipping a beat at the thought that in a day or two she'd be seeing Andrew again.

Between the hospital and Bri, Caitlin was kept busy and was surprised to be paged one day by Dr Sommerville. Her initial flutter of anxiety that the oncologist was phoning with bad news about Brianna was soon dispelled.

'Dr O'Neill,' Antonia said sternly. 'Have you forgotten you have an appointment to see me?'

Caitlin had completely forgotten. Everything that had happened over the last week or so had pushed it out of her mind.

'Would you mind if we reschedule?' she said.

'Are you in the middle of something?'

Caitlin glanced down at the cup of coffee she was holding in her hand. She had seen all her patients and her theatre list wasn't due to start for another hour. The nurse she had been chatting to was within earshot, so Caitlin could hardly lie.

'I'm on my way down right now,' she said, resigned. Her appointment would only take a few minutes and at least it would keep Brianna happy.

But it seemed as she lay on the examination couch, having her breasts examined, that she had misjudged Antonia. The doctor was obviously determined to be thorough. As Caitlin lifted her arms and answered the older woman's questions about her medical history, she let her mind drift to the patients she had scheduled for later.

Her thoughts were interrupted by Antonia

frowning down at her. 'There's a lump here,' she said. 'It's probably nothing but, given your history, I think we should investigate it to be on the safe side. I'd like to do a fine-needle biopsy and send you for a mammogram. Is there any chance you might be pregnant?'

Caitlin's mind was whirling. A lump? She hadn't been aware of anything. Her breasts were usually a little lumpy. Especially around the time of her period. And then just as quickly the thought hit her like a bolt of lightning. But she had missed her period. She was at least five days late. Was it possible that she could be pregnant?

Aware that Antonia was waiting for a reply while she unwrapped the needle she would be using to draw fluid from the lump, Caitlin thought frantically. She'd been on the Pill when she had slept with Andrew. But she had been sick the night she'd returned, and she more than most knew that it could mean she had no longer been protected. And she was never late! She was as regular as clockwork. Perhaps the anxiety over Bri had made her late? But she was beginning to develop a hollow feeling. She had been feeling nauseous the last couple of mornings. It was entirely possible she was pregnant, regardless of how much she wanted to believe otherwise.

'There's a small chance I might be pregnant,' she admitted. 'So until I know for sure, I think we should leave the mammogram.'

Antonio looked at her sharply, but otherwise said nothing. She inserted the needle into the lump and Caitlin grimaced as she withdrew some fluid.

'You can get dressed now,' Antonio said. 'We should have the results for you quite quickly—hopefully by Monday, Tuesday at the latest. I know it's not great to have to wait even a couple of days, but I'll phone you as soon as I have them.' She looked at Caitlin and must have recognised the stunned expression. 'Why don't I leave you here for a while?' she said sympathetically. 'It will give you a bit of time and privacy before you go back to work.' Caitlin nodded mutely and Antonia left her to her thoughts.

Dazed, all Caitlin could think about was the chance she might be pregnant or could have cancer. Either prospect was almost too much to contemplate but together? What if she was pregnant *and* had breast cancer? She knew that treatment for breast cancer was incompatible with pregnancy. And if she did require treatment there was every chance it would make the chances of her ever falling pregnant again remote.

Now that the chances of having children seemed about to be snatched away, Caitlin felt bereft. It was one thing not planning to have children, it was quite another having that decision taken out of her hands.

And if she was pregnant with Andrew's child, how did she feel about that? How would *he* feel about that? Should she even tell him?

Slow down, she told herself. Think it through calmly one step at a time.

Firstly, she told herself, she needed to take a pregnancy test. She would find one down in the clinic. But the last thing she wanted was to draw attention to herself. No, she would stop at the pharmacy on the way home. She would have to wait until that evening before she could take the test. And as for the possibility that the lump

Antonia had found was more than a benign cyst? Well, she would just have to wait for the results of that test too. There was no point in worrying about something that might never happen. She would just need to keep herself busy, which shouldn't be difficult, bearing in mind her busy schedule over the next few days. Then the scientist part of her brain told her that once she had all the facts, then she could decide what to do. Right now she had a job to do, and her patients needed her to be focussed. There would be time later to make decisions.

Caitlin looked at the blue line on the stick and knew her instincts had been correct. She was pregnant. Good going, she thought wryly, for a consultant obstetrician to find herself with an unplanned pregnancy. Surely she of all people could have avoided this? But she hadn't been thinking straight lately. First her concern for Brianna and then her feelings for Andrew had sent her usually ordered mind spinning in all directions. And now that she was faced with the consequences, what was she going to do?

In her head she worked out the dates and how far along her pregnancy was. Although she wasn't far advanced at all she could imagine exactly how the foetus would look at this stage, and she felt the first stirring of protectiveness deep inside her. But she wasn't ready to be a mother. She had her future to think of, her career. Life as a single mother didn't fit into those plans. She shook her head. If the result of the needle biopsy was positive and she needed chemotherapy, she would have to consider terminating the pregnancy anyway. Either that, or not have the treatment and allow the cancer to progress, which it would do more rapidly feeding on the hormones that would be surging around her blood. But although the rational part of her said a termination was a straightforward procedure, something inside of her balked at the idea. How on earth had she, of all people, managed to get herself into this mess?

Brianna tapped on the bathroom door. 'Dinner's ready, Cat.'

Caitlin knew she couldn't stay in the bathroom much longer. Brianna would guess that something was up, and she didn't want to worry her sister. Not when she already had so much on her plate. She wrapped the test in a piece of screwed-up paper and hid it in her pocket. She'd dispose of it later in one of the outside bins. Somehow she'd have to get through the weekend, pretending everything was okay.

But Caitlin had underestimated her sister's perceptiveness. All through Saturday she could feel Brianna's speculative eyes on her and, sure enough, in the evening, while Niall was putting the children to bed, Caitlin found herself cornered.

'Let's take our tea onto the veranda,' Brianna suggested. They sat on the swing seat in companionable silence for a few moments, enjoying the cool evening breeze after the heat of the day. Caitlin was even getting used to the flying ants.

'I have some good news.' Brianna smiled. 'The results of the gene screen came back negative. I know it doesn't mean Siobhan will never get breast cancer, but the odds are more in her favour.'

'I'm so happy for you, Bri. It must be a load off your mind.' Caitlin hugged her sister. It meant that she herself was less likely to have the gene. However, not having the gene didn't mean she didn't have cancer. But she couldn't tell Brianna now, when she looked as if a weight had been lifted from her shoulders. It just wouldn't be fair.

'What is it, Caitlin?' Brianna eventually ventured. 'You're not taking my news with your usual "I told you so." I get the feeling something's up. Is it work? Are you needed back in Ireland? Do you want to go home? Is it Andrew? Something's bothering you for sure. So give.'

'I'm pregnant.' The words slipped out before Caitlin could stop herself. Now she had said them it all seemed so much more real.

'Oh,' Brianna said. Then a few seconds later, 'How do you feel about that?'

'I don't know. That's just it. You know it's not in my plans. At least not right now.'

'Is it David's?'

Caitlin stood and walked across to the edge of the veranda. She laughed shortly. 'No, it's not David's. We hadn't…you know, towards the end, not for a long time. It had all really fizzled out, even before I told him I was coming over here. But I had carried on taking the Pill. Just habit, I guess.'

'Then who…?' Caitlin could hear the sudden realisation in Brianna's voice. 'You don't mean that it's Andrew's? Oh my God, Cat. You do! There's been no one else. I've seen the way you look at him, but I never thought it had got this serious.' She came across and stood next to Caitlin. 'But that's wonderful, isn't it?'

'Wonderful? To be pregnant by a man who doesn't love you? With whom there is no kind of future? Who thinks that women should stay at home, look after the children and be grateful to bring him his slippers at the end of the day? No,' Caitlin said heavily, 'even if he cared for me—which he doesn't, he's made that much clear—Andrew Bedi and I have no future. It's all been a ghastly mistake.'

'Are you going to tell him?' Brianna said quietly. 'Don't you think he has a right to know?'

Caitlin sighed from a place deep in her soul. 'I haven't really decided what to do yet,' she said. 'I don't know if I'm up to bringing up a child on my own. Is it fair, do you think? Me, working all hours, leaving the baby with a child-minder. I don't think that's the kind of life I envisaged for myself.'

She wasn't going to tell Brianna about the lump. There wasn't any point, at least not until Monday when she would get the results. Her sister had been through so much already, it would be unfair to worry her further. She should have kept the pregnancy to herself too, she thought, furious with herself. Why involve Brianna when she didn't have all the facts herself?

Brianna had slumped back in the swing seat, looking dazed. 'You don't mean you'll consider not having it? Oh, Caitlin, think very carefully before you go down that road.'

'I need time to take it all in,' Caitlin said. 'It's all come as a shock. You know me—up until now, up until I came to Australia, my life had been organised, planned down to the last detail. There has never been any room in my life for the unexpected.'

'From that point Australia's been good for you.' Brianna touched Caitlin on the arm. 'You know I hate to say this, Cat, but when you first arrived, I couldn't believe how serious you'd become. You already looked the part of the stereotypical professor. I couldn't see the mischievous Caitlin I remembered anywhere. It's as if you'd had the life sucked out of you.'

Caitlin slid her sister a look. She was horrified but deep down knew her sister was correct. She had been working so hard for so long she had forgotten how to live. Even her relationship with David had been almost, well, convenient. They were two people who shared the same *academic* interests, but that was all. She couldn't remember laughing with David the way she had laughed with Andrew. In fact, she couldn't even remember having fun with David. Not once. The more she thought about it, the more she knew Bri was right. The last few years back in Dublin hadn't really been living. But since she had arrived in Australia, although the circumstances were not what she would have wished, she had never felt so alive. And that's what Andrew made her feel. Alive from the tips of her toes to the top of her head. What on earth was she going to do?

CHAPTER TEN

ANDREW took a sip of his drink and studied the woman opposite him. She was beautiful, with her olive skin and luxuriant mane of hair, as well as being bright and amusing. In short she was everything he thought he wanted in a woman. Why, then, did the image of glittering green eyes and auburn hair keep transposing itself on his thoughts? Why had he been unable to stop thinking of Caitlin and the feel of her silky skin under his fingertips for even a moment?

'I'd love to have children,' Raffia was saying. 'At least half a dozen.'

'What about your degree?' Andrew asked. 'I thought you planned to be a teacher?'

'Only until I have a family,' Raffia replied. 'I do think women should stay at home—if they are lucky enough to be able to afford to. Don't you?'

He did. Or at least he had. Suddenly like a bolt from the blue he realised that something fundamental had changed. He couldn't imagine any sort of life without Caitlin in it. Whatever that life was. What was the point in having children if it wasn't with the woman who made you feel as if your life was complete? Without Caitlin he would only ever be half-alive. Despite his best intentions he had done the very thing he had thought impossible. He had fallen irrevocably in love with the most unsuitable woman. The realisation took his breath away. What a fool he had been. He became aware that Raffia was looking at him curiously.

'You haven't heard a word I've been saying, have you?' she said softly.

'I'm sorry,' he said. 'Please forgive me. But I have to go.' He stood, suddenly desperate to see Caitlin again. He needed to tell her how he felt. Needed to convince her that they should be together. Regardless. If she didn't want children, well, that would be a blow, but maybe he could convince her in time. She could continue working. Women did these days and their children didn't always suffer for it. He might have to do his bit. He pictured himself changing a nappy, his tiny son laughing up at him, and the thought didn't seem quite as ridiculous as it once had. Millions of men, even men he knew like Niall, managed so why shouldn't he?

Raffia was smiling at him. 'You're already in love with someone, aren't you?' she said softly.

Andrew brought himself back to the present. Was it that obvious?

'Yes,' he said. 'How did you know?'

'Oh, we women have a sixth sense as far as these things are concerned. She's a lucky woman.' She smiled ruefully. 'Does she know?'

'No,' Andrew admitted. Then he smiled, knowing that his life was mapped out for better or for worse. That if he had anything to do with it, he had the rest of his life to spend with Caitlin. 'But she will soon.'

'Then don't you think you should find her and tell her?' Raffia suggested.

Andrew bent and kissed her on the cheek. 'I'm sorry… about all this,' he said.

'Hey, don't worry about it.' She giggled. 'The

truth is, I'm sort of seeing someone too. I only agreed to tonight to keep the folks happy, but this way I'll be able to tell them truthfully we weren't right for each other. Now scoot. Before I change my mind.'

On Monday, Caitlin had work as usual. She knew Andrew was back from Sydney and she both dreaded and longed to see him. Arriving early at the hospital, she made her way up to the special care nursery, to check on baby Colin, who had been delivered safely after her initial diagnosis that he might have a heart problem when they had been at the Sunshine Coast clinic. After that, she would go and see Patricia's baby. As it was still early, she hoped to avoid bumping into Andrew. She wasn't ready to see him yet. She was on call for emergencies today, so wouldn't have Outpatients or Theatre.

But as she stepped into the ward she was dismayed to find Andrew lounging against the nurses' station, coffee in hand, laughing at something with one of the nursing staff. At the sight of the familiar features and tall frame, which had haunted her dreams over the last couple of weeks, she felt her heart somersault. Was it possible that he was even more good looking than she remembered? He looked up and caught her eye. A broad grin spread across his face.

'Caitlin,' he said. 'It's good to see you. Have you come to make sure we're looking after your babies?'

He meant baby Colin, but for one horrific second Caitlin thought he knew about the pregnancy. If she decided to tell him, and she wasn't about to, at least not until she knew that she was going to keep the baby, and she was a way off making any decision at all.

'I've been up to see him most days,' she admitted. 'Is he still doing well?'

'Come and see for yourself,' Andrew said. 'We've finished rounds, but I'm sure his parents won't mind another visit from you.'

Baby Colin was indeed continuing to make progress. As Caitlin looked down at the tiny form, still attached to a ventilator but gaining weight and getting stronger every day, she felt her heart shift. She slipped a hand inside the incubator and into a tiny hand. Colin's mouth was like a rosebud. Long lashes lay against delicate cheeks.

'We can't thank you and Dr Bedi enough,' his mother whispered. 'We know without you both our baby could have died.'

'That's what we're here for,' Caitlin said softly. 'It's our job to bring healthy babies into the world and to help those who aren't so healthy survive. It is an honour and a privilege for us to play our part.' She laughed, suddenly self-conscious. She wasn't usually so philosophical. 'But you have the hard part. Eighteen years or more looking after him. Our part was easy in comparison.' She was uncomfortably aware of Andrew's speculative look.

'We'll never forget either of you. Or the nurses. Everyone has been so fantastic,' the husband added. 'You've all made a very stressful time bearable.'

'I'll come in to see you again tomorrow,' Caitlin said. 'In the meantime, Colin's in the best possible hands.'

'Hey,' Andrew said as they walked away, 'is this the *uber*-cool Dr O'Neill showing a softer side? I thought you didn't like to get too involved with your patients? You've been here every day. And to see the Levy baby too, the nurses tell me.'

'I just like to make sure my patients are doing well,' she said defensively. 'That's not the same as being involved.'

Andrew wiggled his eyebrows at her. 'Sure, if that's what you want other people to believe. But you don't fool me. I can see right through that tough exterior.'

Caitlin drew a sharp breath. There was something in the way he was looking at her, as if… She banished the thought. Her hormones were playing up, that was all. She was reading things into situations that didn't exist.

'I was going to look in on baby Levy—little Colleen—on the paeds ward since I'm up this way. Have you seen her since you got back? She's doing fantastically well.'

'Yes,' Andrew said. 'It won't be long before we can discharge her.' He looked at his watch. 'I need to be somewhere,' he said. 'But before I go, how's Brianna? I spoke to Niall on the phone yesterday and he said she's fine. Should I believe him?'

'Why don't you come round this evening and see for yourself?' The words slipped out before Caitlin could stop herself. Once again there was that speculative look in Andrew's eyes.

'Do *you* want me to come?' he asked, his eyes drilling into hers. Caitlin's heart began to gallop in the most uncomfortable way.

'How was the gorgeous mathematician?' she queried instead. Once again the words slipped out before she could stop them.

Andrew's eyes crinkled. 'You're interested? In my love life? I thought you couldn't care less.'

'Of course I don't,' Caitlin retorted. 'Whatever you get up to is up to you. I was only making polite conversation. As one friend to another.'

'Caitlin, I need to speak to you, but in private,' he said. He reached towards her, but before he could say anything more, Caitlin's pager bleeped.

'I need to answer this,' Caitlin said, moving towards the phone. Whatever it was he needed to talk to her about, Caitlin wasn't sure she wanted to hear it. She suspected it had something to do with the woman his mother had lined up for him.

The call was about the woman Caitlin had seen up in Noosa. The one who'd had the positive pregnancy test after IVF. Caitlin's heart sank when the nurse told her that she had presented at the hospital in pain. It sounded ominous to Caitlin.

'I'll be right there,' she said. She turned to Andrew, but he had already gone.

'I'm sorry,' Caitlin told the frightened couple. 'It seems from the scan that you have a twin pregnancy. The trouble is, although one is developing in its proper place, the other is in your Fallopian tube.'

'Can you do anything?' Amy asked shakily.

'I'm sorry,' Caitlin said again, taking Amy's hand in hers. 'I'll have to remove the pregnancy from the tube and possibly the tube itself. The other baby will be fine.'

'But I want them both,' Amy cried. 'I don't want to lose either of my babies.'

Caitlin's heart went out to the young couple.

They wanted these babies so badly. Without thinking, her hand dropped to her own belly. It was early days yet, but the irony wasn't lost on Caitlin. In front of her was a young couple who had fought very hard to have children they desperately wanted. And here she was pregnant without meaning to be, and unsure how she felt about it. For the first time she really thought about the baby growing inside her. What if someone told her she was going to lose it and she might never get pregnant again? How would she feel about that? Then suddenly, sitting in front of the distraught couple, she knew the answer. She wanted this baby. Regardless of how difficult it would make her life, and she was under no illusions as to how difficult her life as a single working mum was going to be, the baby was here now, and for better or worse, if it was at all possible, she was going to keep it. As she made the decision she felt a huge weight lift from her shoulders.

'I know this is difficult for you both, and I know you'll need time later to grieve for the lost baby, but believe me if there was any way to save it I would. And I wish I could give you time to come to terms with it, but I need to operate today. There's a real chance that if we don't, and soon, your tube could rupture, putting your own life in danger. At least, and I know right now it's little compensation, your other baby should be just fine.'

Shaken, Caitlin left the couple in the care of the nursing staff. If she was going to get so involved with every patient, she thought grimly, she'd have nothing left. She realised now why the academic route had seemed so enticing. It had just been another way for her to hide from the harsher realities of life. Being an academic would be so much easier than having to face the difficult emotional issues of her patients every day. But at the same time, Caitlin thought about the babies she had helped save. There was the reward of knowing that she had really made a difference. Although caring brought sadness and pain, it also brought an enormous feeling of satisfaction.

Caitlin kept looking at her watch, wondering when Antonia would call her with the results.

Every hour she had to wait was agonising. Now she knew exactly how her patients felt. Even an hour when you were waiting for important results could seem like an eternity. But when Antonia did page her, it was to tell her that her results wouldn't be back for another couple of days due to a backlog at the lab. She apologised profusely but Caitlin knew that it wasn't her fault. Somehow she would have to get through the next couple of days as best she could.

As she was on call for the labour ward, Caitlin would be staying at the hospital overnight. Brianna's house was simply too far away for her to get back to the hospital quickly enough should an emergency occur and, sure enough, just as she was finishing writing up her notes for the day, her pager bleeped. Caitlin was almost grateful. Anything that would keep her mind occupied was welcome.

It was Dr Hargreaves. 'Ah, Dr O'Neill,' he boomed down the phone. 'I hope I didn't disturb you, but I wondered if you'd like to go with the air ambulance to attend a patient with an unstable lie. If you would, I'll cover the labour suite until you get back.'

'Sure,' Caitlin said. 'I'd like to go.'

'The air ambulance leaves in about ten minutes. There's not much time. The pilot will want to get back before dark if possible. Dr Bedi is going too.'

At the last bit of information Caitlin's heart jumped. On the one hand she didn't want to spend time with him, not until she knew for certain what she was going to do, but on the other hand she was glad it would be Andrew that would be the paediatrician on this, her first callout.

'What about equipment?' she asked.

'Everything you might need will be on the plane,' Dr Hargreaves said. 'Good luck.' And then he hung up.

Caitlin thought quickly. Then she grabbed her stethoscope and white coat. On her way to the pick-up point, she'd collect some scrubs as well.

Andrew was already waiting for her next to the small Cesna. There was no way to talk over the roar of the engines, but Andrew flashed her a smile, before taking her by the elbow and ushering her on board. Inside there was only room enough for the two of them plus an incubator and a stretcher should they need to transport the patient back to hospital. The two seats up front were taken by the pilot, an efficient-looking woman somewhere in her early thirties, and the copilot, an older man with a face like a bloodhound. Andrew introduced them simply as Fran and Steve, and it was obvious that he knew them both well from the easy banter.

Minutes later and they were taking off. Caitlin stared out of the window as they left Brisbane behind. She could see the river snaking like a major artery through the city, crossed by the numerous bridges.

'How far?' she shouted to Andrew, struggling to make herself heard above the noise of the engines.

'About forty minutes,' he replied. 'Just try and relax while you can.'

The noise of the engines made conversation difficult and Caitlin was left alone with her thoughts. She sneaked a look at Andrew, who was sitting with his eyes closed. Once more she felt a mix of emotions. Attraction, there was no denying that, she thought ruefully. She had known she was attracted to him since the first time she had clapped eyes on him, but what she felt was more than physical. She loved being in his company. Life seemed to glitter when he was around. Life just felt more…exciting somehow. But it was no use. If it wasn't for Brianna, Caitlin would be tempted to go back to Ireland and try and get her life under control. But she couldn't. She had promised her sister that she'd be here for six months, only just over a month had passed and she would keep her promise, however difficult she found it. But, she thought, what would happen if she continued with the pregnancy? It would be impossible to keep it from Andrew. What then? She shook her head. Stop it! she told herself. Remember you were going to take one step at a time?

It only seemed like minutes before they were landing. Andrew had passed Caitlin a copy of the woman's notes as they were flying. Just before the plane had started to descend he had brought her up to speed with what he knew about the patient, which he had to admit was very little.

'All we really know is that the nurse is concerned enough to want a doctor on hand,' he had told Caitlin. 'As is often the case, we really don't know exactly what we are dealing with until we get there.'

They jumped out of the plane as soon as Fran said they were free to go. 'There's only an hour before sunset,' she told them, 'and I'd really like to be in the air by then. So I'd appreciate it if you could be as quick as possible.'

The nurse rushed over to meet them. 'Hi, guys. Am I glad to see you,' she said. 'My lady really needs to be in hospital, I think. C'mon, let's take you over. I'm Tanni, by the way.' Then she stopped and looked thoughtful. 'Which one of you is the paediatrician?' she asked.

'That would be me,' Andrew said, as he followed her into the clinic.

'I hoped there would be someone on this flight. I have a two-year-old I'd like you to have a look at when you're finished with Mrs Crouse. It's not an emergency as such. It's just that there is something about him that worries me. And since you're here anyway, it would save him and his parents a long and perhaps unnecessary trip to Brisbane.'

'No probs,' Andrew agreed. 'I'll be happy to have a look just as soon as I'm finished with the woman you called us to see.'

The nurse's fears turned out to be justified. Mrs Crouse's third pregnancy was almost at full term, but the baby was lying bottom first instead of head down. As Caitlin examined her she could tell that the patient was already in advanced labour.

'It's a breech lie,' she told Andrew. 'And her contractions are less than three minutes apart. It's too late to transport her and too late to do a section. We're just going to have to deliver her here.'

Caitlin could tell from Andrew's expression that he recognised the difficult situation their patient was in. If the baby got stuck during labour, and that was a real possibility, they could be dealing with a dead baby. The thought filled Caitlin with dread. She was used to dealing with similar scenarios, but always in fully equipped hospitals. Not in a clinic that was only set up with basic equipment for routine emergencies. But at least, thank God, Andrew was there to help.

But for the time being there was little either of them could do, except wait. While they waited Andrew rummaged through the bag they had brought with them to see what was available.

'I need a paediatric endotracheal tube and a laryngoscope,' Andrew said. 'If the baby's in poor nick, I'll need both.'

Thankfully their search produced both items. At least, if the worst came to the worst and the baby needed resuscitating after delivery, they had the right equipment. Caitlin also found a pair of forceps. Now at least they were as prepared as they could be.

Caitlin felt the women's abdomen. 'Contractions are still around three minutes apart,' she said. 'The baby could come any time. In the next half-hour or not for hours yet. I'm afraid this is just a waiting game now.'

Tanni popped her head back in. 'Could you come and see the child now, Dr Bedi? I'm becoming increasingly concerned about him.'

'Will you be okay here?' Andrew asked Caitlin. 'I'll be as quick as I can.'

Caitlin nodded. 'I'll yell if I need you,' she

said, sitting down next to Mrs Crouse. 'We'll be fine.' She smiled at her patient, who was concentrating on coping with her contractions.

When Andrew returned, Caitlin could see that he was frowning.

'What is it?' she asked. 'Is everything all right?'

'Not really,' he said. 'I'm pretty sure he has meningitis—we need to get him to hospital stat so he can have a lumbar puncture.'

'But Mrs Crouse—Magda—shouldn't be moved,' Caitlin said. 'Why don't you go back with the child while I stay here with Magda? The plane can come back for us.'

'I don't want to leave you on your own. If something goes wrong…' He stared into the distance. 'I think I should send Tanni back with the child. Nothing is going to happen on the flight. I'm confident of that. I'll start him on IV antibiotics just in case. Then once she has seen him admitted she can come back on the flight that picks us up. Dr Hargreaves will just have to stay on until we get back.' He stood, and stretched. 'That's what we'll do,' he said decisively. 'It's not a perfect arrangement, but we'll just have to make the best of it.'

Caitlin nodded. 'You're right. We don't have any other choice.'

Twenty minutes later, they heard the plane take off. Caitlin settled herself by her patient, prepared to wait out the next couple of hours or however long it took for the plane to return. Magda was comfortable enough to close her eyes and fall asleep.

The room they were in was sparsely furnished with a bed and basic monitoring equipment. Apart from one armchair there was only one other uncomfortable-looking plastic orange chair.

Andrew must have noticed her looking indecisive. 'You take the comfy chair if you like. It could be a few hours yet, so get some rest.' But Caitlin was having none of it.

'No. You have it,' she insisted. 'I don't mind.'

Andrew glowered at her. 'Do you have to argue with me about everything, woman?' he said. 'I told you Aussie men don't let their women suffer. Not if they can do anything about it!'

Caitlin felt a frisson run down her spine. Their women? But she wasn't Andrew's woman. He had made that perfectly clear and, besides, she wasn't anybody's woman. She was her own person. She suppressed a smile. Andrew made her feel as if she was in the Wild West. For a moment an image of him tossing her over his shoulder as he walked into the bush, brushing away crocodiles with a disdainful flick of his boot, flashed through her mind, and she felt heat rise from low in her abdomen. God, now he had her thinking the same way. What on earth was happening to her?

'Speaking of which,' she said, 'how was your trip to Sydney?'

'Ah, Sydney,' he said slowly. 'I want to talk to you about that.' He looked down at the sleeping patient. 'But it will have to wait. I don't want an audience. She might wake up at any time.' He looked her in the eye. Could she be mistaken? Or was he looking at her as if, well, as if he cared?

'I'm starving,' he said suddenly. 'It's well past my dinnertime. Why don't I go and see whether I can rustle up something to eat?'

Caitlin didn't really feel like eating. The feeling of nausea that had started on the plane journey was coming back now that she wasn't concentrating her whole attention on her patient.

'I'm not hungry,' she said. 'But why don't you go and get something? I'll shout if I need you.'

But Andrew hadn't been gone long before he was back, holding a couple of plates loaded with food. 'I thought you might be tempted when you smelled it,' he said. But the smell of cooked meat was having the opposite effect on Caitlin. Without warning, her stomach heaved. Covering her mouth with her hand, she rushed over to the basin and was violently sick. Right there. Next to her sleeping patient and in full view of Andrew. Had she not felt as if she were about to die she would have been mortified. Nothing like this had ever happened to her in all the years she had been a doctor. Losing control had never been part of Caitlin's make-up. Until now. She felt a cool hand on her forehead.

'Take it easy,' Andrew said. He waited beside her as she took deep breaths. Eventually the cold sweaty feeling disappeared along with the nausea and she was able to speak. Impatiently she moved away from him.

'I'm sorry you had to witness that,' she said, and slumped down in the armchair.

Andrew moved across the room and knelt by her side. He felt her forehead and then her pulse. 'You should lie down,' he said. 'Perhaps you've picked up the same bug Brianna had.'

'I'm perfectly all right,' Caitlin almost snapped. She would have given anything to be far away from Andrew's searching gaze. 'I'll just splash my face and rinse out my mouth,' she added, starting to rise.

But Andrew was still looking at her, concern deepening his brown eyes. 'If you have some sort of virus, you shouldn't be looking after patients. What if you pass it on?'

'It's not a virus,' Caitlin said before she could stop herself.

Andrew's eyebrows snapped together. 'How can you be so sure?' he asked.

Caitlin was thinking rapidly, unsure of what to do. He was quite right. If she was unwell she shouldn't be around a baby as fragile as this would be. The last thing a premature baby needed was to be exposed to viruses. But she didn't have a virus. She knew exactly what had caused her to be ill. But the last thing she wanted to do was tell him. On the other hand, if she didn't, she would have to excuse herself from the care of the woman and her baby. Could she in all honesty do that?

'I am fine. Please, just trust me on this.'

Andrew narrowed his eyes at her. 'It's all very well to play the martyr,' he said. 'I know we doctors don't like to admit when we are ill, but if it's for the good of our patients, sometimes we have to. So I'm sorry, Cat, you're off the case.'

'Oh, for God's sake, Andrew, I'm pregnant. I've been sick and I'm perfectly all right now.'

He looked at her, stunned. 'Pregnant!' The room was suddenly deathly silent except for the sound of the sleeping woman's breathing. Caitlin watched as emotions chased across Andrew's face. Disappointment, then puzzlement, then slowly a dawning realisation. 'How far on are you?' he asked abruptly.

Caitlin chewed her lip. It was the moment of truth. What should she do? If she led him to believe her pregnancy was more advanced than it was, he'd believe it was David's. That way he would leave her alone. But was that fair? Could she bring herself to tell him an outright lie? On the one hand it would mean that she was free to make her own decision about the pregnancy and he wouldn't have to be involved should she need to make the choice between continuing the pregnancy or, if she had cancer, terminating it. Was it even fair to tell him? Especially when she was certain that should the lump turn out to be malignant she wouldn't want him to know. One thing she knew about Andrew with absolute certainty was that he would feel an obligation towards her if she was pregnant. And an even greater one should she be ill with a possible life-threatening illness. But before she could decide what to say, he stood up and pulled her to her feet. Holding her roughly by her upper arms, he looked her directly in the eye.

'Is it mine?' he demanded. 'For God's sake, Caitlin, tell me. Are you having my baby?'

CHAPTER ELEVEN

IN THE end she couldn't lie and Andrew must have seen the truth in her eyes. They stared at each other in silence.

'I don't think this is the time to talk about this,' Andrew said, indicating their patient with a nod of his head. Caitlin realised that Mrs Crouse was beginning to surface from her sleep, and suddenly she cried out in pain, clutching her stomach.

Quickly, Caitlin bent over to examine Magda. 'I can see a foot,' she called out. 'And a loop of cord.' Then she listened for the baby's heartbeat. 'Foetal heartbeat is dropping. We need to get this baby delivered. Right now!'

She turned to Magda, who was screwing up her eyes in pain.

'Magda, I need you to push. As hard as you can. Do you understand?'

Magda nodded, her eyes wide with fear and pain. Caitlin carefully wrapped her hand around the tiny protruding foot, aware that Andrew was standing by, ready to help. Carefully but firmly she tugged on the foot, acutely conscious that she needed to apply slow but steady pressure. As the baby began to appear she called out. 'Pass me the forceps, Andrew.'

Silently he passed her the forceps and then with a final tug the baby was out. Quickly Caitlin removed the cord from around the baby's neck.

'Two minutes,' Andrew called, holding his arms out to receive the baby, a girl, from Caitlin. It was up to him now. She had done everything she could. Her heart in her mouth, she watched as he placed the still blue form down on the trolley he had prepared earlier and slipped the laryngoscope down the tiny throat. Caitlin sighed with relief as the tube slipped in and Andrew followed it with an endotracheal tube.

'Andrew,' she said as the baby began to pink up, 'don't you think she's a little small for her dates?' The baby should have been a good bit bigger if Mrs Crouse's dates were correct, and then, as Mrs Crouse let out another cry of pain, she locked eyes with Andrew. She knew they were both thinking the same thing.

She whirled around and was just in time to deliver another baby, this time a boy, as Magda gave one final push.

'Did you know you were expecting twins?' she asked the exhausted woman.

'No.' Magda looked astonished. 'I had no idea.'

Caitlin wrapped up the tiny boy and then slipped it in next to Magda. The heat from the mother's skin was the best way to keep the premature infant warm. But at least this one was healthy.

Just as she placed the infant next to his mother, a cry came from where Andrew was working with the baby girl. Caitlin smiled. Somehow she and Andrew had pulled it off and Mrs Crouse had two healthy babies.

Magda was still groggy so Caitlin went over to the cot and picked up the crying infant. As she felt Andrew's eyes on her, the irony of the situation wasn't wasted. Here she was holding a completely helpless baby while inside her was another even more helpless child totally dependent on her as to whether it would live or die. But she couldn't bear to think about it as a baby. She had to think of it as no more than a collection of cells less than a centimetre in diameter. The moment she started to think of it as anything more she'd be lost. It would be too cruel to have to decide whether her life or that of the baby was more important. She felt her eyes fill with tears as she realised it was too late. Whatever she wanted to believe, she knew in her heart of hearts that she had already fallen in love with the tiny life growing inside her. It was hers and Andrew's baby and whatever the future held, she couldn't imagine not having his child.

A short time later, as they finished making Magda and her two babies comfortable, they heard the drone of the plane returning from Brisbane. Looking out of the window, she could see dark clouds had formed overhead, adding to the darkness of the late afternoon, and without warning heavy rain began to lash down. Caitlin jumped as suddenly, without warning, a crack of thunder split the air followed by torrential rain.

'It's a thunderstorm,' Andrew said. 'It'll be

over soon, but it might mean a delay getting back to the hospital.'

More than anything else Caitlin wanted to get away from Andrew. The last thing she wanted was a conversation about the pregnancy. Not yet.

'How long will it last, do you think?' she said, anxiously scanning the dark sky.

'I have no idea,' Andrew said shortly. 'At least Tanni will be back, and as soon as she relieves us we are going to find somewhere quiet so we can finish this conversation. In the meantime, why don't you go and find us some coffee?'

Glad to remove herself from his glowering eyes and formidable expression, Caitlin needed no second bidding. Outside the room she leant against the wall and took deep breaths. There was no doubt in her mind that Andrew intended to finish the discussion they had started. What on earth was going on in his mind? Was he shocked? Don't be stupid, woman, she told herself. Of course he was. Or angry? Probably both. But he had been an equal partner in this mess, she reminded herself. She would make him understand that this was *her* problem. She didn't expect him to play any part.

A flash of sheet lightning was followed closely by a crash of thunder that reverberated around the building. The lights flickered and then moments later went out, plunging Caitlin into darkness. She stood horrified. What if the plane couldn't land? While Magda and her babies were in no immediate danger, the best place for them was in the hospital. And the last thing she needed this evening was a third-degree grilling from Andrew about her pregnancy. But to her relief the power cut only lasted a few seconds, before the electricity supply sprang back into life. Caitlin stood still and watched the progress of the plane as its lights circled over the dusty landing strip.

The next half-hour was spent loading Magda and her babies onto the plane. Caitlin felt immensely thankful there was no opportunity for Andrew to get her on her own. While the pilot carried out last-minute checks, Caitlin took the opportunity to slip back outside and let the now cooling night air wash over her.

She hadn't heard Andrew approach, only becoming aware of him when his hand grasped her arm firmly. He pulled her round to face him, his dark eyes unfathomable in the dim light. She could feel his energy, his intensity surround her like a cloak. Her skin prickled with the tension of being so close to him. She would have given anything to lean into him and let him wash away her fears.

'It is mine, isn't it?' he asked.

She nodded.

She heard him take a deep breath and then he was reaching for her, pulling her into his arms. She could feel his lips on her hair, the softness of his breath in her ear. Too drained to fight him any longer, she leant her body into his, revelling in the feeling of being in his arms. She snuggled into his chest, breathing in the familiar scent of him. If she could have asked for anything right then it would be to stay there for the rest of her life.

'We'll get married,' he said. 'As soon as we can.'

She pulled away from him, feeling the cool wind of their separation. She looked up at him. His dear, puzzled face.

'That's very honourable of you,' she said stiffly, 'but I haven't decided what to do yet.'

He narrowed his eyes. 'What do you mean?' Then he cursed. 'You can't be thinking of getting rid of it? My God, Caitlin, does the thought of having a child, my child, revolt you so much?'

She shook her head at him. 'The timing—' she managed, before he interrupted her.

'You mean that the timing is all wrong? That it will interfere with your career plans? God, Cat.' He tried to pull her back into his arms but she resisted. 'There will be plenty of time for your career when the baby, our baby, is old enough.'

She tried a laugh, but it wasn't very successful. 'You've changed your mind. I thought you disapproved of women who combined motherhood with careers.'

He looked sheepish. Raising his hand, he drew a finger down the contours of her cheek, following the trail to the base of her neck. Caitlin shivered, feeling desire throughout her body. 'I was wrong, okay? I hadn't met you when I thought all that. Now I have…' he laughed, as if astonished '…I realise that being with the right woman, supporting her, is what matters. I couldn't help falling in love with you, and I guess I wouldn't have if you hadn't been you.' He laughed again. 'I'm making a mess of this, aren't I? I guess it's because I have never been in love before.'

In love? Caitlin's mind was reeling. He was in love with her? For a brief moment her heart soared. He loved her and wanted to marry her. She could be with him, grow old with him, share her life with a man who made her world come alive. But then she remembered. She might not have a future. And could she really believe him? What if he was just telling her he loved her to convince her to have his child? And if she told him the truth and she turned out to have cancer, what then? Would he pity her? Stay with her because of a sense of duty? Persuade her to terminate the pregnancy to save her own life and then spend the rest of their lives together, however long that was, resenting her? Even coming to hate her? She could never, ever allow that to happen. She loved him too much. But perhaps, she thought, hope springing, the results would be negative. If that was the case, then they could be together, if she could bring herself to believe he was telling the truth that he loved her. That he didn't want to marry her because of the baby.

He was looking at her expectantly, a small smile playing on his lips. Caitlin took a deep breath, knowing she was about to hurt him deeply.

'I haven't decided what to do about the pregnancy,' she said. 'There's a good chance I may not keep it.' As she said the words she knew it was as if she was stabbing him in the heart. The smile froze on his lips and he drew his brows together. He had never looked so handsome or so frightening to Caitlin before.

'You are a piece of work,' he said at last. 'I have never met a woman like you before.' He laughed bitterly. 'I know you told me your career is important, but I thought you had changed. God, woman, I thought you felt something for me. It just goes to show you how wrong a man could be. I was prepared to go against everything I'd been brought up to believe just to be with you.' He shook his head. 'What a fool.'

Caitlin reached out for him, wanting to tell him the truth. But she let her hand drop to her side. She still thought she might be right. If he couldn't have the baby, then he didn't want her.

'Then I've just prevented you from making the biggest mistake of your life,' she said gently, before turning on her heel and leaving him standing in the darkness.

Later, when Mrs Crouse and her baby had been taken to the ward and Dr Hargreaves relieved, Caitlin made her way tiredly to the on-call room. She had no idea where Andrew had disappeared to, she was simply relieved that they were no longer confined in the small aircraft together.

Wearily she decided against a shower and lay down on the single bed, still in her crumpled theatre greens. It had been a long and emotional night. Her thoughts jumbled around her head. It was all such a mess. If she had known that coming to Australia would throw her life into such turmoil, would she have come? But then she wouldn't have met and fallen in love with Andrew. And while that might have been easier in many, many ways, she would never have known what it was like to be in love. She would have continued through her life, shutting out the world, only half-alive. Whatever happened, she knew that something inside her had changed irrevocably. At the very least she knew she'd be turning down the chair of obstetrics. She would never again seek to hide from life behind papers and research. She would stay with clinical medicine. Her first love. And if she had breast cancer? Well, she would cope with that too. If Bri could get through it, so could she. *And the baby?* the thought whispered in her mind. *What about your baby? Can you really terminate it, even if it means saving your own life?* The thought brought tears to her eyes. How ironic. She had never wanted children and now here she was, possibly having to decide between her own life and that of her unborn child. It was an impossible decision.

She thumped the pillow, rolling over on her side. Please, let her sleep. Let her have a little peace. Just for a while. Perhaps by tomorrow she would know the worst. But she couldn't help the tears from falling when she thought about living the rest of her life without Andrew.

A soft knock on the door woke her from an uneasy sleep. It was still dark and a glance at her watch showed it was just after six in the morning. Caitlin assumed it was someone from the labour ward come to fetch her, but instead when she opened the door it was to find Andrew. He looked dishevelled and haunted. Without waiting for her to invite him in, he strode into the room.

'I've been walking for hours,' he said, keeping his back to her, 'thinking about everything, and it just doesn't make sense.' He turned around and Caitlin could see the lines of anguish around his mouth. 'I *know* you, Caitlin. I've come to know you almost as well as I know myself.' He raked his hand through his hair as he paced the tiny room. Suddenly he looked over at her and Caitlin felt the intensity of his eyes burn into her soul. 'I've watched you with your patients— how dedicated and emotionally involved you are with them, despite yourself. And I know you're not the type of person to have a termination just because a baby is inconvenient.' Caitlin's heart thumped painfully in her chest as she noticed a wave of despair flit across Andrew's face. 'Please, darling,' he whispered hoarsely. 'Tell me. Tell me what's wrong.'

Caitlin couldn't trust herself to speak as she threw herself into his arms. How could she have ever doubted his love? she wondered, feeling Andrew's powerful arms wrapping round her body and holding her tightly, as if he was afraid she would vanish into thin air.

She felt his lips against her hair. 'Please, Caitlin. Tell me what's really troubling you.' He cupped his hand round the back of her neck, letting out a wry laugh. 'I never believed those soppy love songs—but, my God, I'd move heaven and earth for you.'

Caitlin twisted her hands into his shirt. She wanted this moment to last for ever. But she was gaining strength from the love emanating from him, she realised. He had a right to know. And somehow they would face the difficult decisions together.

'I know now why I always told myself I didn't want children,' she mumbled into his chest. 'It was because I saw so much fear and longing with my own patients. It was easier to pretend that that wasn't for me, rather than imagine going through all that heartache. And I thought my career would be enough. But that was before I met you.' She pulled her head back, her eyes searching his. He had the right to know the truth. She took a deep breath. 'Andrew, I might have breast cancer too. That's why I wasn't sure if I could carry on with the pregnancy.' The thought of losing the life inside her welled up again, and Caitlin choked back the tears that were threatening to overwhelm her.

'I love you,' she added, feeling a weight lift from her shoulders. 'I love you more than life itself. I know that now. But this has to be my decision and despite what I said earlier, I don't know if I could go through with a termination.' Caitlin shuddered at the thought.

Before she knew it, Andrew was across the room and lifting the telephone. 'Who is doing the tests for you?' he asked tersely.

'Dr Sommerville,' Caitlin replied. 'But, Andrew, it's only 6.30! You can't get her up...'

'Can't I? Watch me!' His eyes held hers as he waited for the operator to pick up. 'You're not going through another second of this agony, waiting to hear whether you've got cancer or not.' He turned his attention back to the receiver. 'This is Dr Bedi—can you page Dr Sommerville straight away? Yes, yes, I know what time it is, but tell her it's an emergency.' Dropping the phone back in its cradle, Andrew pulled her back into his arms. 'If the test is positive, I'll respect your decision—no matter what it is. All I know is that I want you in my life. Strong and healthy. That's what matters.'

Caitlin attempted a smile. 'Whatever happens, I'm not going to take the post in Ireland. I'm going to live here with you and near Bri. She can help with the baby.' She smiled at the image.

'You'd do all that? For me? Risk your life? Not that there's a chance in hell I'm going to allow you. And give up your career?' He pulled her closer. 'I love you more than I thought it was possible to love a woman.'

'I don't mean give up my career entirely,' she said warningly. 'I have to work, but there's no reason, if you help, that I can't have both.' She snuggled into his arms. And if she had cancer, well, life sometimes dealt a blow. She would just have to take her chances. She knew that even short a life with Andrew was better than a long life without him.

'I suppose I can learn how to change a nappy,' he said. 'Better men than me have managed. Just don't expect me to make a very good job of it.'

Caitlin giggled, imagining his large hands struggling with the fiddly ties of a small nappy. Just then the phone rang. Andrew and Caitlin stared at one another, the air suddenly thick with tension. They both knew it was Dr Sommerville returning Andrew's page. The next few seconds would determine their future—and that of their baby.

Caitlin picked up the phone. She was right. It was Dr Sommerville.

'Oh, Dr O'Neill, I thought it was Dr Bedi who was paging me. It sounded pretty urgent. Switchboard must have put me through to you by mistake.' Before Antonia could end the call, Caitlin interrupted.

'Please, don't go. He was phoning on my behalf. We were wondering whether you had my results. I know it's pretty early to be calling but...' She was aware of Andrew hovering directly behind her. She knew he was perfectly capable of wrestling the phone from her hand.

'Of course. I know you must be anxious. As it happens, I have your results right here. I did try to catch you at home earlier, but Brianna said you were out on a call.'

Suddenly Caitlin couldn't bear to know. If it was bad news, she didn't know if she could hold it together. But for once she had someone to share the burden with. She didn't have to be the strong one all the time. Not any more.

'Antonia,' she said softly, 'I'm going to pass you to Andrew. Could you tell him the results please?'

As she held out the phone to Andrew their eyes locked. As he took the receiver he tipped her face to him.

'I love you,' he said. 'Whatever happens, it's you I want. You will always be enough for me.'

As she returned his steady gaze, she felt his strength flow through her. With him by her side, she could face any thing.

It was only when Andrew replaced the receiver that Caitlin realised she had been holding her breath.

Fear clenched her throat as she noticed tears glistening in Andrew's eyes. Her heart sank. She had cancer. Instinctively, her hand fluttered protectively over her stomach, until she realised Andrew was smiling.

'What…what did she say?' she whispered.

'The tests have come back negative. It's a benign cyst. You're all right. Thank God!'

And then there was no more need for words. Wrapping her arms around him, Caitlin knew she would never live in fear again. With Andrew by her side, and their baby to look forward to, life was going to be a real roller-coaster. And she couldn't wait for it to begin.

MEDICAL™

Large Print

Titles for the next six months…

April

ITALIAN DOCTOR, DREAM PROPOSAL	Margaret McDonagh
WANTED: A FATHER FOR HER TWINS	Emily Forbes
BRIDE ON THE CHILDREN'S WARD	Lucy Clark
MARRIAGE REUNITED: BABY ON THE WAY	Sharon Archer
THE REBEL OF PENHALLY BAY	Caroline Anderson
MARRYING THE PLAYBOY DOCTOR	Laura Iding

May

COUNTRY MIDWIFE, CHRISTMAS BRIDE	Abigail Gordon
GREEK DOCTOR: ONE MAGICAL CHRISTMAS	Meredith Webber
HER BABY OUT OF THE BLUE	Alison Roberts
A DOCTOR, A NURSE: A CHRISTMAS BABY	Amy Andrews
SPANISH DOCTOR, PREGNANT MIDWIFE	Anne Fraser
EXPECTING A CHRISTMAS MIRACLE	Laura Iding

June

SNOWBOUND: MIRACLE MARRIAGE	Sarah Morgan
CHRISTMAS EVE: DOORSTEP DELIVERY	Sarah Morgan
HOT-SHOT DOC, CHRISTMAS BRIDE	Joanna Neil
CHRISTMAS AT RIVERCUT MANOR	Gill Sanderson
FALLING FOR THE PLAYBOY MILLIONAIRE	Kate Hardy
THE SURGEON'S NEW-YEAR WEDDING WISH	Laura Iding

MILLS & BOON®

MEDICAL™

Large Print

July

POSH DOC, SOCIETY WEDDING	Joanna Neil
THE DOCTOR'S REBEL KNIGHT	Melanie Milburne
A MOTHER FOR THE ITALIAN'S TWINS	Margaret McDonagh
THEIR BABY SURPRISE	Jennifer Taylor
NEW BOSS, NEW-YEAR BRIDE	Lucy Clark
GREEK DOCTOR CLAIMS HIS BRIDE	Margaret Barker

August

EMERGENCY: PARENTS NEEDED	Jessica Matthews
A BABY TO CARE FOR	Lucy Clark
PLAYBOY SURGEON, TOP-NOTCH DAD	Janice Lynn
ONE SUMMER IN SANTA FE	Molly Evans
ONE TINY MIRACLE…	Carol Marinelli
MIDWIFE IN A MILLION	Fiona McArthur

September

THE DOCTOR'S LOST-AND-FOUND BRIDE	Kate Hardy
MIRACLE: MARRIAGE REUNITED	Anne Fraser
A MOTHER FOR MATILDA	Amy Andrews
THE BOSS AND NURSE ALBRIGHT	Lynne Marshall
NEW SURGEON AT ASHVALE A&E	Joanna Neil
DESERT KING, DOCTOR DADDY	Meredith Webber

™ MILLS & BOON®